Various Miracles

ALSO BY CAROL SHIELDS

Small Ceremonies

The Box Garden

Happenstance

A Fairly Conventional Woman

Various Miracles
Carol Shields

General — PAPERBACKS —

General Paperbacks edition published in 1989

Published in 1985 by Stoddart Publishing Co. Limited

ISBN 0-7736-7228-1

*The author wishes to thank
the Manitoba Arts Council for its support.*

Printed in U.S.A.

For my daughter Meg

The author and publisher wish to acknowledge with thanks previous publication of the following stories: "Mrs. Turner Cutting the Grass," *Arts Manitoba*, "Dolls, Dolls, Dolls, Dolls," *Aurora/CBC Anthology*, "Sailors Lost at Sea," *Dandelion*, "Purple Blooms," *Quarry*, "Flitting Behavior," *CBC Anthology*, "Various Miracles," *Canadian Forum/Anthology of Prairie Women Writers*, "The Metaphor Is Dead," *Prairie Fire*, "Accidents," "Love So Fleeting," *The Malahat Review*, "Fragility," *Saturday Night*, "Invitations," "The Journal," "Home," *Fiddlehead*, "Salt," *The Antigonish Review*.

Contents

Tell all the truth but tell it slant
> — *Emily Dickinson*

Various Miracles

Various Miracles

SEVERAL OF THE MIRACLES that occurred this year have gone unrecorded.

Example: On the morning of January 3, seven women stood in line at a lingerie sale in Palo Alto, California, and by chance each of these women bore the Christian name Emily.

Example: On February 16 four strangers (three men, one woman) sat quietly reading on the back seat of the number-10 bus in Cincinnati, Ohio; each of them was reading a paperback copy of *Smiley's People*.

On March 30 a lathe operator in a Moroccan mountain village dreamed that a lemon fell from a tree into his open mouth, causing him to choke and die. He opened his eyes, overjoyed at being still alive, and embraced his wife who was snoring steadily by his side. She scarcely stirred, being reluctant to let go of a dream she was dreaming, which was that a lemon tree had taken root in her stomach, sending its pliant new shoots upwards into her limbs. Leaves, blossoms and finally fruit fluttered in her every vein until she began to tremble in her sleep with happiness and intoxication. Her husband got up quietly and lit an oil lamp so that he could watch her face. It seemed to him he'd never really looked at her before and he felt how utterly ignorant he was of the spring that nourished her life. Now she lay sleeping, dreaming, her face radiant. What he saw was a mask of happiness so intense it made him fear for his life.

On May 11, in the city of Exeter in the south of England, five girls (aged fifteen to seventeen) were running across a playing field at ten o'clock in the morning as part of their physical-education program. They stopped short when they saw, lying on the broad gravel path, a dead parrot. He was grassy green in color with a yellow nape and head, and was later identified by the girls' science mistress as *Amazona ochrocephala*. The police were notified of the find and later it was discovered that the parrot had escaped from the open window of a house owned by a Mr. and Mrs. Ramsay, who claimed, while weeping openly, that they had owned the parrot (Miguel by name) for twenty-two years. The parrot, in fact, was twenty-five years old, one of a pair of birds sold in an open market in Marseilles in the spring of 1958. Miguel's twin brother was sold to an Italian soprano who kept it for ten years, then gave it to her niece Francesca, a violinist who played first with the Netherlands Chamber Orchestra and later with the Chicago Symphony. On May 11 Francesca was wakened in her River Forest home by the sound of her parrot (Pete, or sometimes Pietro) coughing. She gave him a dish of condensed milk instead of his usual whole-oats-and-peanut mixture, and then phoned to say she would not be able to attend rehearsal that day. The coughing grew worse. She looked up the name of a vet in the Yellow Pages and was about to dial when the parrot fell over, dead in his cage. A moment before Francesca had heard him open his beak and pronounce what she believed were the words "*Ça ne fait rien.*"

On August 26 a man named Carl Hallsbury of Billings, Montana was wakened by a loud noise. "My God, we're being burgled," his wife, Marjorie, said. They listened, but when there were no further noises, they drifted back to sleep. In the morning they found that their favorite little watercolor — a pale rural scene depicting trees and a winding road and the usual arched bridge — had fallen off the living-room wall. It appeared that it had bounced onto the cast-iron radiator and then ricocheted to a safe place in the middle of the living-room rug. When Carl investigated he found that the hook had worked loose in the wall. He patched the plaster methodically, allowed it to dry, and then installed a new hook. While he worked he remembered how the picture had come into his possession. He had come across it hanging in an emptied-out house in the French city of St. Brieuc, where he and the others of his platoon had been quartered during the last months of the war. The picture appealed to him, its simple lines and the pale tentativeness of the colors. In particular, the stone bridge caught his attention since he had been trained as a civil engineer (Purdue, 1939). When the orders came to vacate the house late in 1944, he popped the little watercolor into his knapsack; it was a snug fit, and the snugness seemed to condone his theft. He was not a natural thief but already he knew that life was mainly a matter of improvisation. Other returning soldiers brought home German helmets, strings of cartridge shells and flags of various sorts, but the little painting was Carl's only souvenir. And his wife, Marjorie, is the only one in the world who knows it to be stolen goods; she and Carl belong to a generation that believes there should be no secrets between married couples. Both of them, Marjorie as much as Carl, have a deep sentimental attachment to the picture, though they no longer believe it to be the work of a skilled artist.

It was, in fact, painted by a twelve-year-old boy named Pierre Renaud who until 1943 had lived in the St. Brieuc house. It was said that as a child he had a gift for painting and drawing; in fact, he had a gift merely for imitation. His little painting of the bridge was copied from a postcard his father had sent him from Burgundy where he'd gone to conduct some business. Pierre had been puzzled and ecstatic at receiving a card from his parent who was a cold, resolute man with little time for his son. The recopying of the postcard in watercolors — later Pierre saw all this clearly — was an act of pathetic homage, almost a way of petitioning his father's love.

He grew up to become not an artist but a partner in the family leather-goods business. In the late summer he liked to go south in pursuit of sunshine and good wine, and one evening, August 26 it was, he and Jean-Louis, his companion of many years, found themselves on a small stone bridge not far from Tournus. "This is it," he announced excitedly, spreading his arms like a boy, and not feeling at all sure what he meant when he said the words, "This is it." Jean-Louis gave him a fond smile; everyone knew Pierre had a large capacity for nostalgia. "But I thought you said you'd never been here before," he said. "That's true," Pierre said, "you are right. But I feel, *here*" — he pointed to his heart — "that I've stood here before." Jean-Louis teased him by saying, "Perhaps it was in another life." Pierre shook his head, "No, no, no," and then, "well, perhaps." After that the two of them stood on the bridge for some minutes regarding the water and thinking their separate thoughts.

On October 31, Camilla LaPorta, a Cuban-born writer, now a Canadian citizen, was taking the manuscript of her new novel to her Toronto publisher on Front Street. She was nervous; the publisher had been critical of her first draft, telling her it relied too heavily on the artifice of coincidence. Camilla had spent many months on revision, plucking apart the faulty tissue that joined one episode to another, and then, delicately, with the pains of a neurosurgeon, making new connections. The novel now rested on its own complex microcircuitry. Wherever fate, chance or happenstance had ruled, there was now logic, causality and science.

As she stood waiting for her bus on the corner of College and Spadina that fall day, a gust of wind tore the manuscript from her hands. In seconds the yellow typed sheets were tossed into a whirling dance across the busy intersection. Traffic became confused. A bus skittered on an angle. Passersby were surprisingly helpful, stopping and chasing the blowing papers. Several sheets were picked up from the gutter where they lay on a heap of soaked yellow leaves. One sheet was found plastered against the windshield of a parked Pontiac half a block away; another adhered to the top of a lamppost; another was run over by a taxi and bore the black herringbone of tire prints. From all directions, ducking the wind, people came running up to Camilla and bringing her the scattered pages. "Oh this is crazy, this is crazy," she cried into the screaming wind.

When she got to the publisher's office he took one look at her manuscript and said, "Good God Almighty, don't tell me, Camilla, that you of all people have become a post-modernist and no longer believe in the logic of page numbers."

Camilla explained about the blast of wind, and then the two of them began to put the pages in their proper order. Astonishingly, only one page was missing, but it was a page Camilla insisted was pivotal, a keystone page, the page that explained everything else. She would have to try to reconstruct it as best she could. "Hmmmmm," the publisher said — this was late in the afternoon of the same day and they sat in the office sipping tea — "I truly believe, Camilla, that your novel stands up without the missing page. Sometimes it's better to let things be strange and to represent nothing but themselves."

The missing page — it happened to be page 46 — had blown around the corner of College Street into the open doorway of a fresh-fruit and vegetable stand where a young woman in a red coat was buying a kilo of zucchini. She was very beautiful, though not in a conventional way, and she was also talented, an actress, who for some months had been out of work. To give herself courage and cheer herself up she had decided to make a batch of zucchini-oatmeal muffins, and she was just counting out the change on the counter when the sheet of yellow paper blew through the doorway and landed at her feet.

She was the kind of young woman who reads everything, South American novels, Russian folk tales, Persian poetry, the advertisements on the subway, the personal column in *The Globe and Mail*, even the instructions and precautions on public fire extinguishers. Print is her way of entering and escaping the world. It was only natural for her to bend over and pick up the yellow sheet and begin to read.

She read: *A woman in a red coat is standing in a grocery store buying a kilo of zucchini. She is beautiful, though not in a conventional way, and it happens that she is an actress who —*

Mrs. Turner
Cutting the Grass

OH, MRS. TURNER is a sight cutting the grass on a hot afternoon in June! She climbs into an ancient pair of shorts and ties on her halter top and wedges her feet into crepe-soled sandals and covers her red-gray frizz with Gord's old golf cap — Gord is dead now, ten years ago, a seizure on a Saturday night while winding the mantel clock.

The grass flies up around Mrs. Turner's knees. Why doesn't she use a catcher, the Saschers next door wonder. Everyone knows that leaving the clippings like that is bad for the lawn. Each fallen blade of grass throws a minute shadow which impedes growth and repair. The Saschers themselves use their clippings to make compost which they hope one day will be ripe as the good manure that Sally Sascher's father used to spread on his fields down near Emerson Township.

Mrs. Turner's carelessness over the clippings plucks away at Sally, but her husband Roy is far more concerned about the Killex that Mrs. Turner dumps on her dandelions. It's true that in Winnipeg the dandelion roots go right to the middle of the earth, but Roy is patient and persistent in pulling them out, knowing exactly how to grasp the coarse leaves in his hand and how much pressure to apply. Mostly they come up like corks with their roots intact. And he and Sally are experimenting with new ways to cook dandelion greens, believing as they do that the components of nature are arranged for a specific purpose — if only that purpose can be divined.

In the early summer Mrs. Turner is out every morning by

ten with her sprinkling can of chemical killer, and Roy, watching from his front porch, imagines how this poison will enter the ecosystem and move by quick capillary surges into his fenced vegetable plot, newly seeded now with green beans and lettuce. His children, his two little girls aged two and four — that they should be touched by such poison makes him morose and angry. But he and Sally so far have said nothing to Mrs. Turner about her abuse of the planet because they're hoping she'll go into an old-folks home soon or maybe die, and then all will proceed as it should.

High-school girls on their way home in the afternoon see Mrs. Turner cutting her grass and are mildly, momentarily repelled by the lapped, striated flesh on her upper thighs. At her age. Doesn't she realize? Every last one of them is intimate with the vocabulary of skin care and knows that what has claimed Mrs. Turner's thighs is the enemy called cellulite, but they can't understand why she doesn't take the trouble to hide it. It makes them queasy; it makes them fear for the future.

The things Mrs. Turner doesn't know would fill the Saschers' new compost pit, would sink a ship, would set off a tidal wave, would make her want to kill herself. Back and forth, back and forth she goes with the electric lawn mower, the grass flying out sideways like whiskers. Oh, the things she doesn't know! She has never heard, for example, of the folk-rock recording star Neil Young, though the high school just around the corner from her house happens to be the very school Neil Young attended as a lad. His initials can actually be seen carved on one of the desks, and a few of the teachers say they remember him, a quiet fellow of neat appearance and always very polite in class. The desk with the initials N.Y. is kept in a corner of Mr. Pring's homeroom, and it's considered lucky — despite the fact that the renowned singer wasn't a great scholar — to touch the incised letters just before an exam. Since it's exam time now, the second week of June, the girls walking past Mrs. Turner's front yard (and shuddering over her display of cellulite) are carrying on their fingertips the spiritual scent, the essence, the fragrance, the aura of Neil Young, but Mrs. Turner is as ignorant of that fact as the girls are that she, Mrs. Turner, possesses a first name — which is Geraldine.

Not that she's ever been called Geraldine. Where she grew up in Boissevain, Manitoba, she was known always — the Lord knows why — as Girlie Fergus, the youngest of the three Fergus girls and the one who got herself in hot water. Her sister Em went to normal school and her sister Muriel went to Brandon to work at Eaton's, but Girlie got caught one night — she was nineteen — in a Boissevain hotel room with a local farmer, married, named Gus MacGregor. It was her father who got wind of where she might be and came banging on the door, shouting and weeping. "Girlie, Girlie, what have you done to me?"

Girlie had been working in the Boissevain Dairy since she'd left school at sixteen and had a bit of money saved up, and so, a week after the humiliation in the local hotel, she wrote a farewell note to the family, crept out of the house at midnight and caught the bus to Winnipeg. From there she got another bus down to Minneapolis, then to Chicago and finally New York City. The journey was endless and wretched, and on the way across Indiana and Ohio and Pennsylvania she saw hundreds and hundreds of towns whose unpaved streets and narrow blinded houses made her fear some conspiratorial, punishing power had carried her back to Boissevain. Her father's soppy-stern voice sang and sang in her ears as the wooden bus rattled its way eastward. It was summer, 1930.

New York was immense and wonderful, dirty, perilous and puzzling. She found herself longing for a sight of real earth which she assumed must lie somewhere beneath the tough pavement. On the other hand, the brown flat-roofed factories with their little windows tilted skyward pumped her full of happiness, as did the dusty trees, when she finally discovered them, lining the long avenues. Every last person in the world seemed to be outside, walking around, filling the streets, and every corner breezed with noise and sunlight. She had to pinch herself to believe this was the same sunlight that filtered its way into the rooms of the house back in Boissevain, fading the curtains but nourishing her mother's ferns. She sent postcards to Em and Muriel that said, "Don't worry about me. I've got a job in the theater business."

It was true. For eight and a half months she was an usherette in the Lamar Movie Palace in Brooklyn. She loved her perky maroon uniform, the way it fit on her shoulders, the way the strips of crinkly gold braid outlined her figure. With a little flashlight in hand she was able to send streams of light across the furry darkness of the theater and onto the plum-colored aisle carpet. The voices from the screen talked on and on. She felt after a time that their resonant declarations and tender replies belonged to her.

She met a man named Kiki her first month in New York and moved in with him. His skin was as black as ebony. *As black as ebony* — that was the phrase that hung like a ribbon on the end of his name, and it's also the phrase she uses, infrequently, when she wants to call up his memory, though she's more than a little doubtful about what *ebony* is. It may be a kind of stone, she thinks, something round and polished that comes out of a deep mine.

Kiki was a good-hearted man, though she didn't like the beer he drank, and he stayed with her, willingly, for several months after she had to stop working because of the baby. It was the baby itself that frightened him off, the way it cried probably. Leaving fifty dollars on the table, he slipped out one July afternoon when Girlie was shopping, and went back to Troy, New York, where he'd been raised.

Her first thought was to take the baby and get on a bus and go find him, but there wasn't enough money, and the thought of the baby crying all the way on the hot bus made her feel tired. She was worried about the rent and about the little red sores in the baby's ears — it was a boy, rather sweetly formed, with wonderful smooth feet and hands. On a murderously hot night, a night when the humidity was especially bad, she wrapped him in a clean piece of sheeting and carried him all the way to Brooklyn Heights where the houses were large and solid and surrounded by grass. There was a house on a corner she particularly liked because it had a wide front porch (like those in Boissevain) with a curved railing — and parked on the porch, its brake on, was a beautiful wicker baby carriage. It was here she placed her baby, giving one last look to his sleeping face, as round and calm as the moon. She walked home, taking her time, swinging her legs. If she had known the word *foundling* — which she didn't — she would have bounded along on its rhythmic back, so airy and wide did the world seem that night.

Most of these secrets she keeps locked away inside her mottled thighs or in the curled pinkness of her genital flesh. She has no idea what happened to Kiki, whether he ever went off to Alaska as he wanted to or whether he fell down a flight of stone steps in the silverware factory in Troy, New York, and died of head injuries before his 30th birthday. Or what happened to her son — whether he was bitten that night in the baby carriage by a rabid neighborhood cat or whether he was discovered the next morning and adopted by the large, loving family who lived in the house. As a rule, Girlie tries not to think about the things she can't even guess at. All she thinks is that she did the best she could under the circumstances.

In a year she saved enough money to take the train home to Boissevain. She took with her all her belongings, and also gifts for Em and Muriel, boxes of hose, bottles of apple-blossom cologne, phonograph records. For her mother she took an embroidered apron and for her father a pipe made of curious gnarled wood. "Girlie, my Girlie," her father said, embracing her at the Boissevain station. Then he said, "Don't ever leave us again," in a way that frightened her and made her resolve to leave as quickly as possible.

But she didn't go so far the second time around. She and Gordon Turner — he was, for all his life, a tongue-tied man, though he did manage a proper proposal — settled down in Winnipeg, first in St. Boniface where the rents were cheap and then Fort Rouge and finally the little house in River Heights just around the corner from the high school. It was her husband, Gord, who planted the grass that Mrs. Turner now shaves in the summertime. It was Gord who trimmed and shaped the caragana hedge and Gord who painted the little shutters with the cut-out hearts. He was a man who loved every inch of his house, the wide wooden steps, the oak door with its glass inset, the radiators and the baseboards and the snug sash windows. And he loved every inch of this wife, Girlie, too, saying to her once and only once that he knew about her past (meaning Gus MacGregor and the incident in the Boissevain Hotel), and that as far as he was concerned the slate had been wiped clean. Once he came home with a little package in his pocket; inside was a diamond ring, delicate and glittering. Once he took Girlie on a picnic all the way up to Steep Rock, and in the woods he took off her dress and underthings and kissed every part of her body.

After he died, Girlie began to travel. She was far from rich, as she liked to say, but with care she could manage one trip every spring.

She has never known such ease. She and Em and Muriel have been to Disneyland as well as Disneyworld. They've been to Europe, taking a sixteen-day trip through seven countries. The three of them have visited the south and seen the famous antebellum houses of Georgia, Alabama and Mississippi, after which they spent a week in the city of New Orleans. They went to Mexico one year and took pictures of Mayan ruins and queer shadowy gods cut squarely from stone. And three years ago they did what they swore they'd never have the nerve to do: they got on an airplane and went to Japan.

The package tour started in Tokyo where Mrs. Turner ate, on her first night there, a chrysanthemum fried in hot oil. She saw a village where everyone earned a living by making dolls and another village where everyone made pottery. Members of the tour group, each holding up a green flag so their tour leader could keep track of them, climbed on a little train, zoomed off to Osaka where they visited an electronics factory, and then went to a restaurant to eat uncooked fish. They visited more temples and shrines than Mrs. Turner could keep track of. Once they stayed the night in a Japanese hotel where she and Em and Muriel bedded down on floor mats and little pillows stuffed with cracked wheat, and woke up, laughing, with backaches and shooting pains in their legs.

That was the same day they visited the Golden Pavilion in Kyoto. The three-storied temple was made of wood and had a roof like a set of wings and was painted a soft old flaky gold. Everybody in the group took pictures — Em took a whole roll — and bought postcards; everybody, that is, except a single tour member, the one they all referred to as the Professor.

The Professor traveled without a camera, but jotted notes almost continuously into a little pocket scribbler. He was bald, had a trim body and wore Bermuda shorts, sandals and black nylon socks. Those who asked him learned that he really was a professor, a teacher of English poetry in a small college in Massachusetts. He was also a poet who, at the time of the Japanese trip, had published two small chapbooks based mainly on the breakdown of his marriage. The poems, sadly, had not caused much stir.

It grieved him to think of that paltry, guarded nut-like thing that was his artistic reputation. His domestic life had been too cluttered; there had been too many professional demands; the political situation in America had drained him of energy — these were the thoughts that buzzed in his skull as he scribbled and scribbled, like a man with a fever, in the back seat of a tour bus traveling through Japan.

Here in this crowded, confused country he discovered simplicity and order and something spiritual, too, which he recognized as being authentic. He felt as though a flower, something like a lily, only smaller and tougher, had unfurled in his hand and was nudging along his fountain pen. He wrote and wrote, shaken by catharsis, but lulled into a new sense of his powers.

Not surprisingly, a solid little book of poems came out of his experience. It was published soon afterwards by a well-thought-of Boston publisher who, as soon as possible, sent him around the United States to give poetry readings.

Mostly the Professor read his poems in universities and colleges where his book was already listed on the Contemporary

Poetry course. He read in faculty clubs, student centers, classrooms, gymnasiums and auditoriums, and usually, partway through a reading, someone or other would call from the back of the room, "Give us your Golden Pavilion poem."

He would have preferred to read his Fuji meditation or the tone poem on the Inner Sea, but he was happy to oblige his audiences, though he felt "A Day At The Golden Pavilion" was a somewhat light piece, even what is sometimes known on the circuit as a "crowd pleaser." People (admittedly they were mostly undergraduates) laughed out loud when they heard it; he read it well, too, in a moist, avuncular amateur actor's voice, reminding himself to pause frequently, to look upward and raise an ironic eyebrow.

The poem was not really about the Golden Pavilion at all, but about three midwestern lady tourists who, while viewing the temple and madly snapping photos, had talked incessantly and in loud, flat-bottomed voices about knitting patterns, indigestion, sore feet, breast lumps, the cost of plastic raincoats and a previous trip they'd made together to Mexico. They had wondered, these three — noisily, repeatedly — who back home in Manitoba should receive a postcard, what they'd give for an honest cup of tea, if there was an easy way to remove stains from an electric coffee maker, and where they would go the following year — Hawaii? They were the three furies, the three witches, who for vulgarity and tastelessness formed a shattering counterpoint to the Professor's own state of transcendence. He had been affronted, angered, half-crazed.

One of the sisters, a little pug of a woman, particularly stirred his contempt, she of the pink pantsuit, the red toenails, the grapefruity buttocks, the overly bright souvenirs, the garish Mexican straw bag containing Dentyne chewing gum, aspirin, breath mints, sun goggles, envelopes of saccharine, and photos of her dead husband standing in front of a squat, ugly house in Winnipeg. This defilement she had spread before the ancient and exquisitely proportioned Golden Pavilion of Kyoto, proving — and here the Professor's tone became grave — proving that sublime beauty can be brought to the very doorway of human eyes, ears and lips and remain unperceived.

When he comes to the end of "A Day At The Golden Pavilion" there is generally a thoughtful half second of silence, then laughter and applause. Students turn in their seats and exchange looks with their fellows. They have seen such unspeakable tourists themselves. There was old Auntie Marigold or Auntie Flossie. There was that tacky Mrs. Shannon with her rouge and her jewelry. They know — despite their youth they know — the irreconcilable distance between taste and banality. Or perhaps that's too harsh; perhaps it's only the difference between those who know about the world and those who don't.

It's true Mrs. Turner remembers little about her travels. She's never had much of a head for history or dates; she never did learn, for instance, the difference between a Buddhist temple and a Shinto shrine. She gets on a tour bus and goes and goes, and that's all there is to it. She doesn't know if she's going north or south or east or west. What does it matter? She's having a grand time. And she's reassured, always, by the sameness of the world. She's never heard the word *commonality*, but is nevertheless fused with its sense. In Japan she was made as happy to see carrots and lettuce growing in the fields as she was to see sunlight, years earlier, pouring into the streets of New York City. Everywhere she's been she's seen people eating and sleeping and working and making things with their hands and urging things to grow. There have been cats and dogs, fences and bicycles and telephone poles, and objects to buy and take care of; it is amazing, she thinks, that she can understand so much of the world and that it comes to her as easily as bars of music floating out of a radio.

Her sisters have long forgotten about her wild days. Now the three of them love to sit on tour buses and chatter away about old friends and family members, their stern father and their mother who never once took their part against him. Muriel carries on about her children (a son in California and a daughter in Toronto) and she brings along snaps of her grandchildren to pass round. Em has retired from school teaching and is a volunteer in the Boissevain Local History

Museum, to which she has donated several family mementos: her father's old carved pipe and her mother's wedding veil and, in a separate case, for all the world to see, a white cotton garment labeled "Girlie Fergus' Underdrawers, handmade, trimmed with lace, circa 1918." If Mrs. Turner knew the word *irony* she would relish this. Even without knowing the word irony, she relishes it.

The professor from Massachusetts has won an important international award for his book of poems; translation rights have been sold to a number of foreign publishers; and recently his picture appeared in the *New York Times*, along with a lengthy quotation from "A Day At The Golden Pavilion." How providential, some will think, that Mrs. Turner doesn't read the *New York Times* or attend poetry readings, for it might injure her deeply to know how she appears in certain people's eyes, but then there are so many things she doesn't know.

In the summer as she cuts the grass, to and fro, to and fro, she waves to everyone she sees. She waves to the high-school girls who timidly wave back. She hollers hello to Sally and Roy Sascher and asks them how their garden is coming on. She cannot imagine that anyone would wish her harm. All she's done is live her life. The green grass flies up in the air, a buoyant cloud swirling about her head. Oh, what a sight is Mrs. Turner cutting her grass and how, like an ornament, she shines.

Accidents

AT HOME MY WIFE IS MODEST. She dresses herself in the morning with amazing speed. There is a flashing of bath towel across the fast frame of her flesh, and then, *voilà*, she is standing there in her pressed suit, muttering to herself and rummaging in her bag for subway tokens. She never eats breakfast at home.

But the minute we hit the French coast — we stay in a vacation flat owned by my wife's brother-in-law — there she is, on the balcony with her bare breasts rising up to the sun. And she has breakfasted, and so have I, on three cups of coffee and a buttered croissant.

Her breasts have remained younger than the rest of her body. When I see her rub them with oil and point them toward the fierce sunlight, I think of the Zubaran painting in the museum at Montpellier which shows a young and rather daft-looking St. Agatha cheerfully holding out a platter on which her two severed breasts are arranged, ordinary and bloodless as jam pastries.

One morning something odd happened to my wife. She was sitting on the balcony working on her new translation of Valéry's early poems and she had a cup of coffee before her. I should explain that the dishes and cutlery and cooking things in the flat are supplied, and that this particular coffee cup was made of a sort of tinted glass in a pattern which can be found in any cheap chain store in France. Suddenly, or so she told me later, there was a cracking sound, and her cup lay in a thousand pieces in the saucer.

It had simply exploded. She wondered at first if she had been shot at with an air rifle. There was another apartment building opposite under construction, and at any time of the day workmen could be seen standing on the roof. But clearly it would have required an extraordinary marksman to pick off a cup of coffee like that from such a distance. And when she sifted through the slivers of glass, which she did with extreme care, she found no sign of a pellet.

The incident unnerved her. She put on her blouse when she went out on the balcony later in the day, but I noticed she kept a cup of coffee in the middle of the table as though daring a second explosion to occur.

I knew, though I'm not a scientist, that occasionally tempered glass fractures spontaneously. It's thought to come about by a combination of heat, light and pressure. It happens sometimes to the windshields of automobiles, though it is extremely rare and not entirely understood.

I told all this to my wife. "I still don't understand how it could have happened," she said. I explained again, knowing my explanation was vague and lacking in precision. I was anxious to reassure her. I reached down and put my arms around her, and that was how my accident occurred. She turned to look at me, and as she did so, the back of her earring tore the skin of my face.

It was surprising how long the tear was, about four inches in all, and it was deeper than just a scratch, although the blood oozed out slowly, as though with reluctance. We both realized I would require stitches.

The doctor in the Montpellier clinic spoke almost perfect English, but with a peculiar tonelessness, rather like one of those old-fashioned adding machines clicking away. "You will require a general anesthetic," he told me. "You will be required to remain in the hospital overnight."

My wife was weeping. She kept saying, "If only I hadn't turned my head just at that moment."

The doctor explained that since the hospital was full, I would have to share a room. Always, he said, gesturing neatly with both hands, always at vacation time there were accidents. A special government committee, in fact, had been established to look into this phenomenon of *accidents des vacances*, and someone had suggested that perhaps it might be the simplest solution if vacations were eliminated entirely.

I speak French fluently, having grown up in Montreal, but I have difficulty judging the tone of certain speakers. I don't know when someone — the doctor, for example — is speaking ironically or sincerely; this has always seemed to me to be a serious handicap.

While still under the anesthetic I was put into a room occupied by a young man who had been in a motorcycle accident. He had two broken legs and a shattered vertebra and was almost completely covered in white plaster. Only his face was uncovered, a young face with closed eyes and smooth skin. I put my hand on my own face which was numb beneath the dressing, and wondered for the first time if I would be left with a scar.

My wife came to sit by my bed for a while. She was no longer crying. She had, in fact, been shopping and had bought a new pale-yellow cardigan with white flowers around the neck, very fresh and springlike. I was touched to see that she had removed her earrings. On her ear lobes there was nothing but a faint dimple, the tiny holes made, she once told me, by her own mother when she was fourteen years old.

There seemed little to talk about, but she had bought a *Herald Tribune,* something she normally refuses to do. She scorns the *Herald Tribune,* its thinness and its effete news coverage. And it's her belief that when you are in another country you should make an attempt to speak and read the language of that country. The last time she allowed herself to buy a *Herald Tribune* was in 1968, the week of Trudeau's first election.

The young man with the broken legs was moaning in his sleep. "I hope he doesn't go on like this all night," she said. "You won't get any sleep at this rate."

"Don't worry about me," I said. "I'll be fine tomorrow."

"Do you think we should still plan to go over to Aigues Mortes?" she asked, naming the place we try to visit every summer. Aigues Mortes is, as many people have discovered, an extraordinary medieval port with a twelfth-century wall in near-perfect condition. It has become a habit with my wife and me to go there each year and walk around this wall briskly, a distance of two kilometers. After that we take a tour through the Tower of Constance with an ancient and eccentric guide, and then we finish off the afternoon with a glass of white wine in the town square.

"It wouldn't feel like a holiday if we didn't do our usual run to Aigues Mortes," my wife said in a rather loud cheerful voice, the sort of voice visitors often acquire when they come to cheer the sick.

The man with the broken legs began to moan loudly and, after a minute, to sob. My wife went over to him and asked if she could do anything for him. His eyes were still closed, and she leaned over and spoke into his ear.

"Am I dead?" he asked her in English. "Did you say I was dead?"

"Of course you aren't dead," she said, and smiled over her shoulder at me. "You're just coming out of the anesthetic and you're not dead at all."

"You said I was dead," he said to her in clear carrying British tones. "In French."

Then she understood. "No, we were talking about Aigues Mortes. It's the name of a little town near here."

He seemed to need a moment to think about this.

"It means *dead waters*," my wife told him. "Though it's far from dead."

This seemed to satisfy him, and he drifted off to sleep again.

"Well," my wife said, "I'd better be off. You'll be wanting to get to sleep yourself."

"Yes," I said, "that damned anesthetic, it's really knocked me for a loop."

"Shall I leave you the *Herald Tribune*?" she asked, "or are you too tired to read tonight?"

"You take it," I told her, "unless there's any Canadian news in it."

That's another thing we don't like about the *Herald Tribune*. There's hardly ever any news from home, or if there is, it's condensed and buried on a back page.

She sat down again on the visitor's chair and drew her cardigan close around her. In the last year she's aged, and I'm grieved that I'm unable to help her fight against the puckering of her mouth and the withering away of the skin on her upper arms. She went through the paper page by page, scanning the headlines with a brisk professional eye. "Hmmm," she said to herself in her scornful voice.

"Nothing?" I asked.

"Well, here's something." She folded back the page and began to read. "Gilles Villeneuve is dead."

"Who?"

"Gilles Villeneuve. You know, the racing driver."

"Oh?"

"Let's see. It says Canadian racing driver, killed in practice run. Et cetera. Always claimed racing was dangerous and so on, said a year ago that he'd die on the track." She stopped. "Do you want to hear all this?"

"No, that's enough." I felt the news about Gilles Villeneuve calmly, but I hope not callously. I've never really approved of violent sports, and it seems to me that people foolish enough to enter boxing rings or car races are asking for their own deaths.

"It's sad to die so young," my wife said as if required to fill the silence I'd left.

The young man in the next bed began to sputter and cough, and once again my wife went over to see if she could do anything.

"You mustn't cry," she said to him. She reached in her bag for a clean tissue. "Here, let me wipe those tears away."

"I don't want to die." He was blubbering quite noisily, and I think we both felt this might weaken the shell of plaster that enclosed him.

My wife — I forgot to mention that she is still a very beautiful woman — placed her hand on his forehead to comfort him.

"There, there, it's just your legs. You've been sleeping and you're only a little bit confused. Where do you come from?"

He murmured something.

"What did you say?"

"Sheffield. In England."

"Maybe I can telephone someone for you. Has the hospital sent a message to your people?"

It was an odd expression for her to use — *your people*. I don't think I've ever heard her use that particular phrase before.

"It's all right," he said. He had stopped crying, but my wife kept her hand on his forehead for another moment or two until he had dropped off to sleep.

I must have dropped off to sleep as well because when I opened my eyes she had gone. And after that it was morning and a nurse was opening the shutters and twittering something at me in French. The bed next to mine was empty, and she began to strip off the sheets.

"Where is he?" I asked her in my old formal schoolboy French. "Where's my comrade with the broken legs?"

"Il est mort," she said in the same twittering singsong.

"But he can't be dead. His legs were broken, that's all."

"The spinal cord was damaged. And there were other injuries. Inside."

A minute later the doctor came in and had a look under my dressing. "You perhaps will have a little scar," he said. "For a woman this is terrible, of course. But for a man..." He smiled and revealed pink gums. "For a man it is not so bad."

"I understand that he's died," I said, nodding at the stripped bed.

"Ah yes. Multiple injuries, there was no hope, from the moment he was brought in here yesterday."

"Just a young man," I said.

He was pressing the bandage back into place. "*Les accidents des vacances*. Every year the same. What can one do. One should stay home, sit in the garden, be tranquil."

When my wife comes for me in half an hour or so, I will

have prepared what I'll say to her. I know, of course, that the first thing she'll ask me is: how is the young man from Sheffield? She will ask this before she inquires about whether I've had a good night or whether I'm suffering pain. I plan my words with precision.

This, luckily, is my métier, the precise handling of words. Mine is a profession that is close to being unique; at least I know of no one else who does the same sort of work on a full-time basis.

I am an abridger. When I tell people, at a party for instance, that I am an abridger, their faces cloud with confusion and I always have to explain. What I do is take the written work of other people and compress it. For example, I am often hired by book clubs to condense or abridge the books they publish. I also abridge material that is broadcast over the radio.

It's a peculiar profession, I'm the first to admit, but it's one I fell into by accident and that I seem suited for. Abridging requires a kind of inverse creativity. One must have a sharp eye for turning points and a seismic sensitivity for the fragile, indeed invisible, tissue that links one event with another. I'm well-paid for my work, but I sometimes think that the degree of delicacy is not appreciated. There are even times when it's necessary to interfere with the truth of a particular piece, and, for the sake of clarity and balance, exercise a small and inconspicuous act of creativity which is entirely my own. I've never thought of this as dishonesty and never felt that I had tampered with the integrity of a work.

My wife will be here soon. I'll watch her approach from the window of my hospital room. She still walks with a kind of boyish clip-clop, as though determined to possess the pavement with each step. This morning she'll be wearing her navy blazer; it's chilly, but probably it will warm up later in the day. Probably she'll have her new yellow cardigan on underneath, but I won't be able to tell from here if she's wearing earrings. My guess is that she won't be. In her hand she'll have a small cloth bag, and I can imagine that this contains the picnic we'll be taking with us to Aigues Mortes.

"And how is *he*?" she's going to ask me in a few minutes from now. "How is our poor young friend with the broken legs?"

"He's been moved to a different place." I'll say this with a small shrug, and then I'll say, quickly, before she has a chance to respond, "Here, let me carry that bag. That's too heavy for you."

Of course it's not heavy at all. We both know that. How could a bag containing a little bread and cheese and perhaps two apples be heavy?

It doesn't matter. She'll hand me the bag without a word, and off we'll be.

Sailors Lost at Sea

ONE AFTERNOON, out of curiosity or else boredom, Hélène wandered into an abandoned church. A moment later she found herself locked inside.

This was in France, in Brittany, and Hélène was a girl of fourteen who had been walking home from the village school to the house where she and her mother were temporarily living. Why she had stopped and touched the handle of the church door, she didn't know. She had been told, several times, that the little church was kept tightly locked, but today the door had opened easily at her touch. This was puzzling, though not daunting, and she had entered bravely, holding her head high. She had recently, since arriving in France, come to understand the profit that could be had from paying attention to good posture, how she could, by a minor adjustment of her shoulders or a lifting of her chin, turn herself into someone who had certain entitlements.

She and her mother were from Canada and, despite her Manitoba accent — which she knew seemed quaint, even comic to French ears, funnier even than Québécois — she was regarded with envy and awe by the girls in the village school in St. Quay. That she was from a place called Winnipeg, the girls found exotic. "Weenie-pegg," they said, with a giggling way of hanging on to the final "g." Her mother said this was because St. Quay was an out-of-the-way sort of place.

This was true. It was a fact that only two girls in her level had ever been to Paris, which was just five hours away by train, and a surprising number of them had never been even as far as

Rennes. Also impressive to these girls was the fact that Hélène's mother was a poet, a real poet, who had published three books. *Trois livres? Vraiment?* Their eyes had opened wide at this and they weren't giggling any longer. ("That's one thing about the French," Hélène's mother told her, "they respect writers.") The girls at l'école Jeanne d'Arc were forever asking Hélène how her mother was getting on with her poetry. *"Ta mère, elle travaille bien?"* Their own mothers were the wives of fishermen or shopkeepers. Hélène had been presented to some of these mothers in the village streets; thick-ankled, round-faced women wearing old woolen coats and carrying groceries in bags made of plastic net.

Hélène and her mother had never intended to spend the whole of the year in St. Quay. They had planned to travel, to drift like migrants along the edges of the country. *(La France has the shape of a hexagon, Hélène has been taught in the village school; this fact is repeated often, as though it carries mystical significance.)* Instead of traveling, they had attached themselves like barnacles — this was how Hélène's mother put it — to this quiet spot on the channel coast, and Hélène had enrolled in the local school. There was a very good reason for this, her mother surprised her by saying. "The only way to get the feel of the country is to become a part of it." Of course, as Hélène now knew, and as her mother would soon discover, it was not possible at all for them to become part of the community. Everywhere they went, to the boulangerie, to the post office, everywhere, there was a rustle and a whisper that went before them, announcing, just behind the weak smiles of welcome, "Ah, les Canadiennes!" It made Hélène feel weak; she always was having to compose herself, to imagine how she must look from the outside.

In St. Quay there were a number of old churches, though the largest, a church dating from the thirteenth century, had been torn down ten years earlier. It had been replaced with a brown brick building which was square and ugly like a factory, and distressingly empty, distressing, that is, to the local priest, a Father Dominic. He was an old man with creased yellow skin and a stiff manner, but he was the only friend Hélène's mother had so far found in St. Quay.

"Alas," said Father Dominic, rubbing his long chin, "Brittany was once the most religious corner of France, and now it has become, overnight" — he made a zigzag in the air to signify lightning — "*secularized.*" He said this in his loud, lonely voice, speaking as though there could be no reversal.

"The church," he said, "had lost out to television and motorbikes and modernism in general, and it had all happened in a flash."

Well, this was not quite the truth, Hélène's mother explained later. The truth was that during the French Revolution Brittany had been filled with ranting anticlerical mobs who tore the statues out of church niches and removed stone chunks (heads chiefly or the fingers of upraised hands) from the roadside cavalries that dotted the Côte du Nord. *Quel dommage*, Hélène's mother said in sly imitation of Father Dominic, her only friend.

The particular church where Hélène found herself imprisoned on a Thursday afternoon was one of these small, desecrated churches, statueless and plain, its heavy doors shorn clean of carving and its windows replaced by dull opalescent glass. The church was officially closed. She knew that; it had been closed for many years.

Father Dominic had explained to them that it was no longer served by a priest. Nowadays there was but a single mass celebrated here each year — it was he who had the privilege of serving — and that was on a certain spring day set aside by tradition to honor sailors who had been lost at sea. On that particular Sunday in early April, the doors would be thrown open and people would enter carrying armloads of spring flowers; after that, a procession would wind over the rocks and down the beach itself.

When Hélène's mother heard Father Dominic talking about this festival, her eyes had softened with feeling and she had nodded as though she, too, had had occasion to pay tribute to lost seamen — which, of course, coming from Winnipeg, she had not.

"That will be something to see," she said to Hélène, and wrote the name of the festival in her notebook. At that moment, seeing her mother writing down the details of the fête and imagining the blond sunniness of this festive day, Hélène truly understood that they would be staying here the entire year, that their drifting, which she had loved, all ten days of it, was not to be resumed.

The old church stood just outside the village on the rue des Chiens, the same street where they had found a house to rent. "We've installed ourselves in a cheap stone house on Dog Street." Hélène's mother had written this in a cheerful letter to a friend back home, as though having an inelegant address gave them an unconquerable ascendancy over the difficulties the little stone house presented. There it stood, surrounded by drenched shrubbery, a dragging lace of rain falling from the corners of the steep roof. The landlord, a scowling, silent widower with three teeth in his head, lived in the basement, and his presence cast a spell of restraint over them so that they tiptoed about the house, *his* house, in bedroom slippers and spoke to each other in hushed formal voices, more like a pair of elderly sisters than a mother and daughter. The bathroom stank despite the minty blue deodorizer Hélène had bought and attached to the wall, and the kitchen was damp and without cupboards. The two armchairs in the living room were covered with ancient, oily tapestry cloth, badly frayed. In the morning her mother made coffee, carried it to one of these repellent chairs, and sat down with her notebooks. There she spent her time, scarcely getting up and looking out at the sea all day. Hélène knew without asking that the poems were not coming easily.

By good fortune the Canadian government had seen fit to award her mother a sum of money so that she could come to France for a year in order to write poetry. She had long desired — and this was explained at great length in the application —

to touch the soil where her ancestral roots lay. (But these roots, she now admitted to Hélène in one of their long whispered talks, were more deeply buried than she had thought. Her forebears had gone to Canada a long time ago, first to Quebec, then making their way to Manitoba.) And she was not entirely certain which region of France they had come from, though it was generally believed to have been either Brittany or Normandy. Now she was here, breathing French air, eating French bread, drinking bitter black coffee and taking weekend walks on the wild wetted path that went along the coast, but what really was the use of this? What had she expected? For the so-called roots to rise up and embrace her?

It seemed to Hélène that her mother had childish notions about the magic of places. A field of oats was a field of oats. The blackberries they'd found along the coast path had the same beaded precision as those at home. Her mother had a way of making too much of things, always seeing secondary meanings, things that weren't really there, and her eyes watered embarrassingly when she spoke of these deeper meanings. It was infantile, the way she went on and on about the *fond* of human experience. What was the *fond* but carrying home the groceries, trying to keep warm in the drafty stone house, walking down the dark road in the morning to school where the other girls waited for her, admiring her warm wool sweaters and asking her how her mother, the poet, was doing.

Recently Hélène's mother, as if to make up for the lack of poems, had latched with fevered intensity on to particles of local lore, prising them out of Michelin guides and storing them up in notebooks — not the same notebooks the poems went into, but pale green spiral-bound books with squared-off pages, notebooks (meant for young school children) that she bought in the village at the Maison de la Presse. In one of these notebooks, she had recorded:

There are two legends surrounding the founding of St. Quay, stories that contain similar elements but that occupy different sides of a coin. In the "good" story, a fourth-century Irish saint called St. Quay arrives in a stone boat to bring Christianity to the wild Breton coast. A bird flies ahead to tell the villagers of his imminent arrival, and the women (why just women?) joyfully run to the shore to greet him, bringing with them armloads of flowers and calling "St. Quay, St. Quay," guiding the boat to safety with their cries.

In the second version, the "bad" version, the same bird arrives to say that a stranger is approaching in a stone boat. The women (women again!) of the village are suspicious and hostile, and they run to the shore with rough stalks of gorse in their hands which they brandish ferociously, all the time crying, "*Quay, quay*," which means in old Gaelic, "Away, away."

Her mother asked Hélène one day which version she preferred, but before Hélène could decide, she herself had said, "I think the second version must be true." Then she qualified. "Not true, of course, not in a real sense, but containing the elements, the *fond* of truth."

"Why?" Hélène had asked. She saw the shine on her mother's face and felt an obligation to keep it there. "Why not the first version?"

"It's a matter of perspective," her mother said. "It's just where I am now. In my life, I mean. I can believe certain things but not others."

Because of the way she had said this, and the way she had squeezed her eyes shut, Hélène knew her mother was thinking about Roger, the man in Winnipeg she was in love with. She had been in love before, several times. Love, or something like it, was always happening to her.

But now something had happened to Hélène; she was locked inside a church, chosen somehow, the way characters in stories are chosen. The thought gave her a wavelet of happiness. And a flash of guilty heat. She should not have entered the door; it should not have been unlocked and she should not be standing

here — but she was. And what could she do about it —
nothing. The feeling of powerlessness made her calm and
almost sleepy. She looked about in the darkness for a place
to sit down. There was nothing, no pews, no chairs, only the
stone floor.

She tried the door again. The handle was heavy and made
of some dull metal that filled her hand. She set her school
bag on the floor and tried turning the handle and pushing
on the door at the same time, leaning her shoulder into the
wood. Then she pulled the door toward her, rattled it sharply
and pushed it out again.

"Open," she said out loud, and heard a partial echo float
to the roof. It contained, surprisingly, the half-bright tone of
triumph.

"I'm fourteen years old and locked in a French church."
These words slid out like a text she had been asked to read
aloud. Calm sounds surrounded by their own well of calm; this
was a fact. It was no more and no less than what had happened.

Perhaps there was another door. She began to look around.
The windows, high up along the length of the church, let in
soft arches of webbed light, but the light was fading fast. It
was almost five o'clock and would be dark she knew, in half
an hour. Her mother would be waiting at home, the kitchen
light on already, something started for supper.

High overhead was a dense, gray collision of dark beams
and stone arches, and the arches were joined in such a way
that curving shadows were formed, each of them like the
quarter slice out of a circle. Hélène had made such curves
with her pencil and compass under the direction of Sister
Ste. Adolphe at the village school, and had been rewarded
with a dainty-toothed smile and a low murmur, "*Très, très
bon.*" Sister Ste. Adolphe gave her extra pencils, showed her
every favor, favors that, instead of exciting envy among the
girls, stirred their approval. Hélène was a foreigner and
deserved privileges. It was unjust.

It occurred to Hélène that there must be a reason for the
church to be open. Perhaps there was a workman about or

perhaps Father Dominic himself had come to see that the church was safe and undisturbed during its long sleep between festivals.

"Hello," she called out. *"Bonjour.* Is there anyone here?" She stood still, pulling her coat more closely around her and waiting for an answer.

While she waited, she imagined two versions of her death. She would be discovered in the spring when the doors were flung open for the festival. The crowds, rushing in with armloads of flowers, would discover what was left of her, a small skeleton, odorless, as neat on the floor as a heap of stacked kindling, and the school bag nearby with its books and pencils and notebooks would provide the necessary identification.

Or some miracle of transcendence might occur. This was a church, after all, and close by was the sea. She might be lifted aloft and found with long strands of seaweed in her hair; her skin would be bleached and preserved so that it gleamed with the lustre of certain kinds of shells, and her lips, caked with salt, would be parted to suggest a simple attitude of prayerfulness. (She and her mother, in their ten days of wandering, had visited the grave of an imbecile, a poor witless man who had lived as a hermit in the fourteenth century. It was said, a short time after his death and burial, that a villager had noticed a golden lily growing from the hermit's grave, and when the body was exhumed it was discovered that the bulb of the plant was located in his throat, a testimonial to his true worth and a rebuke to those who had ignored him in his life.)

It occurred to Hélène that her mother would blame herself and not France. Lately, she was always saying, "One thing about France, the coffee has real flavor." Or, "At least the French aren't sentimental about animals," or "You can say one thing for France, things are expensive but quality is high." It seemed her mother was compelled to justify this place where she had deliberately settled down to being lonely and uncomfortable and unhappy.

It had all been a mistake, and now her mother, though she didn't say it, longed for home and for Roger. "A man friend" is what she called Roger, saying this phrase with special emphasis as though it was an old joke with a low wattage of energy left in it. Roger loved her and wanted to marry her. They had known each other for two years. His first wife left him. "He's very bitter," Hélène's mother said, "and for someone like Roger, this can be a terrible blow, a great humiliation."

He was a chef at the Convention Center in downtown Winnipeg. When he was a young man, he was taken into the kitchens of the Ritz Carleton in Montreal where he learned sauces and pastries and salads. He learned to make sculptures out of butter or lard or ice or sugar, and even — for it was an arduous apprenticeship, he tells Hélène — how to fold linen table napkins in twenty classic folds. Would she like a demonstration? She had said yes, despising herself, and Roger had instantly obliged, but he could remember only thirteen of the twenty ways. Now, at the Convention Center, he seldom does any cooking himself, but supervises the kitchen from a little office where he spends his time answering the phone and keeping track of grocery orders.

On Saturday nights he used to come to the apartment in St. Vital where Hélène and her mother lived, and there in the tiny kitchen he made them veal in cream or croquettes or a dish of steamed fish, pickerel with white mushrooms and pieces of green onion.

"Tell me what you like best," he'd say to Hélène, "and next week I'll try it out on you."

Of course, he often stayed the night. He was astonishingly neat, never leaving so much as a toothbrush in the bathroom. On Sunday mornings he made them poached eggs on toast — ducks in their nests he calls them. He had a trick with the eggs, lifting them from the simmering water with a spatula, then flipping them onto a clean, cotton tea towel, patting them dry, and then sliding them onto buttered triangles of toast — all this without breaking the yolks. He learned to do this at the Ritz Carleton when he was a young man. "It would not have been acceptable," he said," to serve an egg that was *wet*." He does it all very quickly and lightly, moving like a character in a speeded-up movie. The first time he did it for Hélène — she was only twelve at the time — she had clapped her hands, and now he's made it into a ceremony, one of several that has unsettled the household.

"Come here, little duckie," he says, flashing his spatula. "Turn yourself over like a good little duck for Hélène." Hélène, when he said this, found it hard to look at her mother, who laughed loudly at this showmanship, her mouth wide and crooked.

Later, after Roger had left, there were a few minutes of tender questioning between them. Hélène's mother, settling down on the plumped cushions, talked slowly, evenly, taking, it would seem, full measure of the delicate temperamental balance of girls in their early adolescence. About the disruption to the household, she was apologetic, saying, "This is only temporary." And, saying with her eyes, "This is not how I planned things." ("Shhh," she said to Roger when he became too merry, when he was about to tell another joke or another story about his apprenticeship.) "How do you like Roger?" her mother asked her. Then, instead of waiting for an answer, her mother began to talk about Roger's ex-wife, how vicious she had been, how she left him for another man.

"I hope I'm not barging in," Roger said, if he dropped by in the middle of the week. He was always bringing presents, not just food, but jewelry, once an alarm clock, once a coat for her mother and a silk blouse for herself. ("I don't know what girls like," he'd said abjectly on this occasion. "I can take it back.")

This is what made Hélène numb. She couldn't say a word in reply, and her silence ignited a savage shame. What was the matter? The matter was that they were waiting for her. They were waiting for her to make up her mind, just as the girls in the schoolyard with their *cartables* and their regulation blouses wait for her to arrive in the dark mornings and bring some improbable substance into the cement schoolyard. "Tell us about Weenie-pegg. Tell us about the snow."

It was growing very cold inside the church, but then even the churches they had visited in September had been cold. Hélène and her mother had carried cardigans. "You can never tell about the weather here," her mother had said, puzzled. This was a point scored against France, a plus for Manitoba where you at least knew what to expect.

And soon it would be dark. Frail moons of light pressed like mouths on the floor, though the walls themselves were darkly invisible. Hélène reached out and rubbed her hand along the rough surface. This was — she began to figure — this was a fourteenth-century church; twenty centuries take away fourteen — that left six; that meant this church was 600 years old. She and her mother had visited churches that were even older, some that went back a thousand years — but now, for the first time, she felt herself seized by the depth and windiness of time. Here she was, enclosed by walls that were 600 years old, walls that were planted by the side of a road called rue des Chiens in a village called St. Quay, which was hidden away in the hexagon that was France. And her body would not be found until spring.

O Mother of God, she said to herself, and rubbed at her hair. O Mother of Jesus.

She tried the door again, putting her ear to the wood to see if she could sound out the inner hardware. There was only a thickish sound of metal butting against wood and the severed resistance of moving parts. She was going to perish. Perish. At fourteen. The thought struck her that her mother would never get over this. She would go back home and tell Roger she couldn't marry him. She would stop writing poems about landscapes that were "jawbone simple and picked clean by wind" and about the "glacé moon pinned like a brooch in the west." She would sink into the *fond* and her mouth would sag open — this was not how she had planned things. And who's fault was it?

By now the church was entirely dark, but at the far end the altar gleamed dully. It seemed a wonder to Hélène that she could summon interest in this faint light. What was it? There was no gold or ornamentation, only a wooden railing that had been polished or worn by use, and the last pale light lay trapped there on the smooth surface like a pool of summer water.

O Mother of God, she breathed, thinking of Sister Ste. Adolphe, her tiny teeth.

She ran her hand along its edge. There was something else at one end. Altar candles. The light didn't reach this far, but her hand felt them in the darkness, a branched candle holder, rising toward the center. She counted the tall candles with her fingers. Up they went like little stairs, one, two, three, four, five, six and then down again on the other side.

There might be matches, she thought, and fumbled at the base of the candle holder. Then she remembered she had some in her school bag. Her mother had asked her to stop at the *tobagie* for cigarettes and matches. (At home in St. Vital they had refused to sell cigarettes to minors, but here in France no one blinked an eye; a point for France.)

She felt her way back to where she left the bag, rummaged for the matches, and then moved back along the wall to the candles. She managed to light them all, using only three matches, counting under her breath. The stillness of the flames seemed of her own creation, and a feeling of virtue struck her, a ridiculous steamroller. She thought how she would never again in her life be able to take virtue seriously.

Astonishing how much light twelve candles gave off. The stone church shrank in the light so that it seemed not a church at all, but a cheerful meeting room where any minute people might burst through the door and call out her name.

And, of course, that was what would happen, she realized. The lit-up church would attract someone's notice. It was a black night and rain was falling hard on the roof, but nevertheless someone — and soon — would pass by and see the light from the church. An immediate investigation would be in order. Father Dominic would be summoned at once.

This might take several minutes; he would have to find his overshoes, his umbrella, not to mention the key to the church. Then there would be the mixed confusion of embracing and scolding. How could you? Why on earth? Thank God in all his mercy.

Until then, there was a width of time she would enter and inhabit. There was nothing else she could do; it was laughable. All she had to do was stand here warming her hands in the heat of the twelve candles — how beautiful they were really! — and wait for rescue to come.

Purple Blooms

THERE IS A BOOK I like by the Mexican poet Mario Valeso who, by coincidence, lives here in this city and who, in the evening, sometimes strolls down this very street. The book is entitled *Purple Blooms* and it is said to resolve certain perplexing memories of the poet's childhood. It is a work that is full of tact, yet it is tentative, off-balance, dark and truncated — and it is just this lack of finish that so moved me the first time I read it.

I gave a copy of the book to my friend, Shana, who's been "going through a bad time," as she puts it. People who meet her generally are struck by her beauty. She's young, well-off and in excellent health, yet she claims that the disconnectedness of life torments her. Everything makes her sad. Lilacs make her sad. Chopin makes her sad. The thought of rain falling in a turbulent and empty ocean makes her sad. But nothing makes her sadder than the collection of toby jugs that her mother, the film actress, left her in her will.

More than a hundred of these sturdy little creatures fill the shelves of her sunny apartment. I myself find it unnerving the way they glisten and grin and puff out their pottery cheeks as though oblivious to the silly pouring lip that deforms the tops of their heads. Knick-knacks, Shana calls them, willfully denying their value, but she refuses nevertheless to part with them, though I've given her the name of an auctioneer who would guarantee a fair price.

It could be said that she encourages her sadness. It could be demonstrated. On her glass-topped coffee table she keeps a large vase of lilacs and an alabaster bust of Chopin and, since last Saturday, my gift of Mario Valeso's book *Purple Blooms*. The denseness, the compaction of the closed text and the assertive angle with which it rests on the table suggest to me that she has not yet opened its pages.

I also have given a copy to Edward. He is attractive, my Edward. I've spent a considerable number of hours staring at him, hoping his handsome features would grow less perfect, more of a match for my own. What does he see in me? (This is the question I ask myself — though I like to think I put it rhetorically.)

"*Purple Blooms*," Edward murmured as he slipped the gift wrap off the book, and then he said it again — *Purple Blooms* — in that warm, sliding, beet-veined voice of his. His father, as everyone knows, sang tenor with the Mellotones in the late forties, and some say that Edward has inherited something of the color of his voice. Edward, of course, vehemently denies any such inheritance. When he hears old records of "Down by the Riverside" or "I'm Blue Turning Gray Over You" he cannot imagine how he came to be the son of such a parent. The line of descent lacks distinction and reason, and Edward is a distinguished and reasoning man. He is also a man attentive to the least sexual breeze, and the minute he pronounced the words, "*Purple Blooms*," I began worrying that he would find the poems not sensual enough for his liking.

"These poems are about the poet's past," I explained to Edward, rather disliking myself for the academic tone I was taking. "Valeso is attempting to make sense of certain curious family scenes that have lingered in his memory."

Edward, wary of dark sublimities, examined the dust jacket. "It won't bite you," I said, joking. He placed the book in his briefcase and promised he would "look at it" on the weekend or perhaps on his summer holidays.

"If you're not going to read it," I said, testing him, "I'll give it to someone else."

For a minute we were pitched straight into one of those little arched silences that lean inward on their own symmetry as though no exterior force existed. Edward took my hand sweetly, then rubbed his thumb across the inside of my wrist, but I noticed he did not promise me anything, and that made me uneasy.

As always, when I'm uneasy, I go out and buy my mother a present. Sometimes I bring her roasted cashews or fresh fruit, but today I take her a copy of *Purple Blooms*. "A book?" she shouts. She has not read a book since she was a young girl.

Fat and full of fury, she stands most days by an upstairs window and spies on the world. What possible need does she have for books, she asks me. Life is all around her.

To be more truthful, life is all behind her. At eighteen she was crowned North America's Turkey Queen at Ramona, California and wore a dress that was entirely made up of turkey feathers. She has the dress still, though I've never laid eyes on it since she stores it in a fur vault in San Diego, once a year mailing off a twelve-dollar check for storage fees and saying, as she drops the envelope in the mailbox, "Well, so much for misspent youth."

How I plead with her! Go to a movie, I say. Invite the neighbors in. Take a course in French conversation or gourmet cooking or music appreciation. A year ago she stopped the newspapers. When the picture tube went on the TV, she decided it wasn't worth fixing. It seems nothing that's happening in the world has any connection with the eighteen-year-old girl carried so splendidly through the streets of Ramona with a crown of dusky turkey feathers in her hair.

"What do I want with a book about flowers," my mother growls. Her tone is rough, though she loves me dearly. I explain that the book is not about flowers (and at the same time imagine myself slyly trading on her innocent error at some future gathering of friends). "This poet," I tell her, "is attempting to recall certain early scenes which bloomed mysteriously and darkly like flowers, and which he now wants to come to terms with."

This is rather an earful for my mother. She pulls at her apron, looks frowningly at the ceiling, then out the window;

this last I recognize as a signal that she wants me to leave, and I do.

Later that afternoon I find myself in the park. Almost everyone knows about the very fine little park at 16th and Ossington — a gem of a park with a wide gravel path and a sprightly round-headed magnolia and smooth painted benches by the side of a bowling green. A cool, quiet place to sit and read, but today it is filled with people.

I stop and ask some schoolchildren what the excitement is about, and a little boy in a striped sweater tells me that Mario Valeso is autographing copies of *Purple Blooms* over in the shady spot under the magnolia tree. There is a great deal of pushing and shoving and general rowdyism. Everyone, it seems, has brought along a copy of *Purple Blooms* for Mr. Valeso to sign. Shana is there with Edward, her arm slipped through his, and they both tell me they have "been greatly helped and strengthened" by reading the poems. "It's all a matter of making connections," Shana says in her breathless way, and Edward says, "It's discovering that we all share the same ancestors."

Then, to my surprise, I catch sight of my mother ahead of me in the crowd, and it pleases me to see she has put on her best cardigan and her white shoes and that she is holding forth loudly to someone or other, saying, "Letting go of the past means embracing the present." Someone else is saying, "The seeds of childhood grow on mysterious parental soil," and an old man in a baseball cap is muttering, "We are the sum of our collective memories."

The crowd grows even larger, and again and again I find myself pushed to the end of the line. I realize it will be hours before my turn comes, and so I pull a book out of my knapsack to help while away the time. It is a new book of poetry, untitled and anonymous, which appears to be a celebration of the randomness and disorder of the world. We are solitary specks of foam, the poet says, who are tossed on a meaningless sea. Every wave is separate, and one minute in time bears no relationship to the moment that precedes or follows it.

I read on and on, and soon forget about the people crowding around me and reading over my shoulder. The bowling green fades into dimness, as do the benches and the magnolia tree and the gravel path, until all that's left is a page of print, a line of type, a word, a dot of ink, a shadow on the retina that is no bigger, I believe, than the smallest violet in the woods.

Flitting Behavior

SOME OF MEERSHANK'S wittiest writing was done during his wife's final illness.

"Mortality," he whispered each morning to give himself comfort, "puts acid in the wine." Other times he said, as he peered into the bathroom mirror, "Mortality puts strychnine in the candy floss. It puts bite in the byte." Then he groaned aloud — but only once — and got straight back to work.

His novel of this period, *Malaprop In Disneyfield*, was said to have been cranked out of the word processor between invalid trays and bedpans. In truth, he wept as he set down his outrageous puns and contretemps. The pages mounted, 200, 300. The bulk taunted him, and meanwhile his wife, Louise, lingered, her skin growing as transparent as human skin can be without disintegrating. A curious odor, bitter and yellow, stole over the sickroom. Meershank had heard of the odor which preceded death; now he breathed it daily.

It was for this odor, more than anything else, that he pitied her, she who'd busied herself all her life warding off evil smells with scented candles and aerosol room fresheners. Since a young woman she'd had the habit of sweetening her bureau drawers, and his too, with sprigs of dried lavender, and carrying always in her handbag and traveling case tiny stitched sachets of herbs. He had sometimes wondered where she found these anachronistic sachets; who in the modern industrial world produced such frivolities? — the Bulgarians maybe, or the Peruvians, frantic for hard currency.

Toward the end of Louise's illness he had a surprise visit

from his editor, a vigorous, leggy woman of forty who drove up from Toronto to see how the new manuscript was coming along. She came stepping from her car one Monday afternoon in a white linen jumpsuit. Bending slightly, she kissed Meershank on both cheeks and cried out, "But this is extraordinary! That you can even think of work at a time like this."

Meershank pronounced for her his bite-in-the-byte aperçu, very nearly choking with shame.

He was fond of his editor — her name was Maybelle Spritz — but declined to invite her into his wife's bedroom, though the two women knew and liked each other. "She's not strong enough for visitors," he said, knowing it was the smell of the room he guarded her from, his poor Louise's last corner of pride. "Maybe later."

He and Maybelle sat drinking coffee on the veranda most of the afternoon. The weather all week had been splendid. Birds sang in the branches of Meershank's trees, and sunlight flooded the long triangle of Meershank's side lawn. Maybelle, reading slowly as always, turned over the manuscript pages. Her nails were long and vivid. She held a pencil straight up in her hand, and at least once every three minutes or so she let loose a bright snort of laughter which Meershank welcomed like a man famished. He watched her braided loop of auburn hair and observed how the light burned on the tips of her heavy silver earrings. There was a bony hollow at the base of her neck that deepened, suddenly, each time another snort was gathering. Later, at five o'clock, checking his watch, he offered gin and tonic. For Louise upstairs he carried cream of celery soup, weak tea and an injection for her hip, which the visiting nurse had taught him to administer.

"Are you feeling lonely?" his wife asked him, turning on one side and readying herself for the needle. She imagined, rightly, that he missed her chatter, that her long days spent in drugged sleep were a deprivation. Every day she asked the same question, plunging him directly into blocky silence. Yes, he was lonely. No, he was not lonely. Which would please her more? He kept his hand on her discolored hip and mumbled the news

— testing it — that Maybelle Spritz was thinking of coming for a visit.

She opened her eyes and managed a smile as he rearranged the pillows. He had a system: one pillow under each knee, one at the small of her back and two to support her shoulders. The air in the room was suffocating. He asked again, as he did every day, if he might open a window. No, she said, as she always did; it was too cold. She seemed convinced that spring had not arrived in its usual way, she who'd always been so reasonable.

Downstairs Maybelle stood in the kitchen drinking a second gin and tonic and heating up a noodle pudding she had brought along. She had occasionally been a dinner guest in Meershank's house, but had never before penetrated the kitchen. She set a little table on the veranda. There was a breeze, enough to keep the mosquitoes away for a bit. Knives and forks; she discovered them easily in the first drawer she opened. The thick white dinner plates she found stacked on a shelf over the sink. There were paper napkins of a most ordinary sort in a cupboard. As she moved about she marveled at the domesticity of the famous, how simple things appeared when regarded close up, like picking up an immense orange and finding it all thick hide on a tiny fruit. She wondered if Meershank would ask her to spend the night.

They had only once before shared a bed, and that had been during the awful week after Louise's illness had been diagnosed.

The expression *terminal*, when the doctor first pronounced it, had struck Meershank with a comic bounce, this after a lifetime of pursuing puns for a living. His scavenger self immediately pictured a ghostly airline terminal in which scurrying men and women trotted briskly to and fro in hospital gowns.

The word *terminal* had floated out of the young doctor's wide pink face; it was twice repeated, until Meershank collected himself and responded with a polite nod. Then he put back his head, counted the ceiling tiles — twelve times fourteen — and decided on the spot that his wife must not be told.

The specialist laced clean hands across flannel knees and pressed for honest disclosure; there were new ways of telling people that they were about to die; he himself had attended a recent symposium in Boston and would take personal responsibility...

No. Meershank held up his hand. This was nonsense. Why did people insist that honesty was the only way of coping with truth? He knew his wife. After thirty-five years of marriage he knew his wife. She must be brought home from the hospital and encouraged to believe that she would recover. Rest, medication, country air — they would work their healing magic. Louise could always, almost always, be persuaded to follow a reasonable course.

The following day, having signed the release papers and made the arrangements to have his wife moved, Meershank, until then a faithful husband, took his editor, Maybelle Spritz, to a downtown hotel and made plodding love to her, afterward begging pardon for his age, his grief, and his fury at the fresh-faced specialist who, concluding their interview, had produced one of Meershank's books, *Walloping Westward*, and begged the favor of an inscription. Meershank coldly took out a pen and signed his name. He reminded himself that the Persians had routinely put to death the bearer of bad news.

Home again, with Louise installed in the big front bedroom, he resumed work. His word processor hummed like a hornet from nine to five and the pages flew incriminatingly out of the printer. During the day his brain burned like a lightbulb screwed crookedly into a socket. At night he slept deeply. He wondered if he were acquiring a reputation for stoicism, that contemptible trait! Friends stopped by with gifts of food or flowers. The flowers he carried up to Louise's bedroom where they soon drooped and died, and the food he threw in the garbage. Coffee cakes, almond braids, banana loaves — his appetite had vanished.

"Eat," Maybelle commanded, loading his plate.

He loved noodle pudding, and wondered how Maybelle

knew. "It's in your second novel," she reminded him. "*Snow Soup and Won Ton Drift*. Remember? Wentzel goes into the cafe at Cannes and demands that —"

"I remember, I remember." Meershank held up a hand. (He was always holding up a hand nowadays, resisting information.) He had a second helping, injecting starch and sweetness. This was hardly fitting behavior for a grieving husband. He felt Maybelle's eyes on him. "I shoulda brought more," she said, sounding for a minute like a girl from Cookston Corners, which she was. "I said to myself, he'll be starving himself."

For dessert he rummaged in the refrigerator and found two peaches. Louise would have peeled them and arranged the slices in a cut glass bowl. Meershank and Maybelle sat eating them out of their hands. He thought to himself: this is like the last day of the world.

"Ripe," Maybelle pronounced. There was a droplet of juice on her chin, which she brushed away with the back of her hand. Meershank observed that her eyes looked tired, but perhaps it was only the eye shadow she wore. What was the purpose of eye shadow, he wondered. He had never known and couldn't begin to imagine.

A character in his first book, *Swallowing Hole*, had asked this question aloud to another character, who happened to be his wife. What was her name? Phyllis? Yes, Phyllis of the phyllo pastry and philandering nights. "Why do you smudge your gorgeous green eyes with gook?" he, the cockolded husband, had asked. And what had the fair Phyllis replied? Something arch, something unpardonable. Something enclosing a phallic pun. He had forgotten, and for that he blessed the twisted god of age. His early books with their low-altitude gag lines embarrassed him and he tried hard to forget he had once been the idiot who wrote them.

Maybelle, on the other hand, knew his oeuvre with depressing thoroughness and could quote chapter and verse. Well, that was the function of an editor, he supposed. A reasonable man would be grateful for such attention. She was a good girl. He wished she'd find a husband so he would feel less often that she'd taken the veil on his account. But at least she didn't expect him to converse with wit. Like all the others, she'd bought wholesale the myth of the sad jester.

It was a myth that he himself regarded with profound skepticism. He'd read the requisite scholarly articles, of course, and had even, hypocrite that he was, written one or two himself. Humor is a pocket pulled inside out; humor is an anguished face dumped upside down; humor is the refuge of the grunting cynic, the eros of the deprived lover, the breakfast of the starving clown. Some of these cheap theories he'd actually peddled aloud to the graduating class at Trent a year ago, and his remarks had been applauded lustily. (How much better to lust applaudingly, he'd cackled, sniggered, snorted inside his wicked head.)

He suspected that these theories were leapt upon for their simplicity, their symmetry, their neat-as-a-pin ironic shimmer. They were touted by those so facile they were unable to see how rich with ragged comedy the world really was. But Meershank knew, he knew! Was it not divinely comic that only yesterday he'd received a telephone solicitation from the Jackson Point Cancer Fund? Wasn't it also comic that the specter of his wife's death should fill him with a wobbly lust for his broad-busted, perfume-wafting, forty-year-old editor? For that matter, wasn't it superbly comic that a man widely known as a professional misogynist had remained happily married to one woman for thirty-five years? (Life throws these kinky curves a little too often, Meershank had observed, and the only thing to do was open your fool mouth and guffaw.)

At nine he checked once again on his wife, who was sleeping quietly. If she woke later, a second injection was permitted. He carried a bottle of brandy out on to the veranda. One for the road, he asked Maybelle with his eyebrows. Why not, she said with a lift of her shoulders. Her upper lip went stiff as a ledge in the moonlight and he shuddered to think he was about to kiss her. The moon tonight was bloated and white, as fretful as a face. Everywhere there was the smell of mock-orange blossoms which had bloomed early this year and in absurd profusion. Crickets ticked in the grass, like fools, like drunkards. Meershank lifted his glass. The brandy burned his throat and made him retreat for an instant, but Maybelle became attenuated, lively, sharp of phrase, amusing. He laughed aloud for the first time in a week, wondering if the world would crack down the middle.

It did. Or seemed to. A loud overhead popping noise like the cracking of whips made him jump. Maybelle slammed down her glass and stared. All around them the sky flashed white, then pink, then filled with rat-a-tat-tat fountains and sparks and towering plumes.

"Jesus," Maybelle said. "Victoria Day. I almost forgot."

"I did forget," Meershank said. "I never once thought."

A rocket whined and popped, made ropy arcs across the sky, burst into petals, leaving first one, then a dozen blazing trails. It was suddenly daylight, fierce, then faded, then instantly replaced by a volley of cracking gunpowder and new showers of brilliance.

The explosions, star-shaped, convulsive, leaping one out of the other, made Meershank think of the chains of malignant cells igniting in his wife's body.

He set down his brandy, excused himself, and hurried upstairs.

Meershank, marrying Louise Lovell in 1949, had felt himself rubbing bellies for the first time with the exotic. He, a Chicago Jew, the son of a bond salesman, had fallen in love with a gentile, a Canadian, a fair-haired girl of twenty who had been gently reared in the Ottawa Valley by parents who lived quietly in a limestone house that was a hundred years old. It faced on the river. There was a rose garden crisscrossed by gravel paths and surrounded by a pale-pink brick wall. Oh, how silently those two parents had moved about in their large square rooms, in winter wrapping themselves in shawls, sitting before pots of raspberry-leaf tea and making their good-natured remarks about the weather, the books they were forever in the middle of, the tiny thunder of politics that flickered from their newspaper, always one-day-old.

The mother of Louise possessed a calm brow of marble. The father had small blue eyes and hard cheeks. He was the author of a history of the Canadian Navy. It was, he told Meershank, the *official* history. Meershank was given a signed copy. And he was given, too, with very little noise or trouble, the hand of Louise in marriage. He had been stunned. Effortlessly, it seemed, he'd won from them their beloved only daughter, a girl of soft hips and blond hair done roundly in a pageboy.

"What exactly do you do?" they only once asked. He worked as a correspondent for a newspaper, he explained. (He did not use the word *journalist*.) And he hoped one day to write a book. ("Ah! A book! Splendid!")

The wedding was in the month of June and was held in the garden. Meershank's relatives did not trouble to travel all the way up from Chicago. The wedding breakfast was served out-of-doors, and the health of the young couple — Meershank at twenty-seven was already starting to bald — was toasted with a non-alcoholic fruit punch. The family was abstemious; the tradition went back several generations; alcohol, tobacco, caffeine — there wasn't a trace of these poisons in the bloodstream of Meershank's virgin bride. He looked at her smooth, pale arms — and eventually, when legally married, at her smooth pale breasts — and felt he'd been singularly, and comically, blessed.

There is a character, Virgie Allgood, in Meershank's book, *Sailing to Saskatchewan*, who might be said to resemble Louise. In the book, Virgie is an eater of whole grains and leafy vegetables. Martyrlike, she eschews French fries, doughnuts and liver dumplings, yet her body is host to disease after disease. Fortified milk fails. Pure air fails. And just when the life is about to go out of her, the final chapter, a new doctor rides into town on a motorbike and saves her by prescribing a diet of martinis and cheesecakes.

There is something of Louise, too, in the mother in

Meershank's tour-de-force, *Continuous Purring*. She is a woman who cannot understand the simplest joke. Riddles on cereal boxes have to be laboriously explained. Puns strike her as being untidy scraps to be swept up in a dustpan. She thinks a double entendre is a potent new drink. She is congenitally immune to metaphor (the root of all comedy, Meershank believes) and on the day her husband is appointed to the Peevish Chair of Midbrow Humor, she sends for the upholsterer.

When *Encounter* did its full length profile on Meershank in 1981, it erred by stating that Louise Lovell Meershank had never read her husband's books. The truth is she not only had read them, but before the birth of the word processor she typed them, collated the pages, corrected their virulent misspelling, redistributed semicolons and commas with the aplomb of a goddess, and tactfully weeded out at least half of Meershank's compulsive exclamation points. She corresponded with publishers, arranged for foreign rights, dealt with book clubs and with autograph seekers, and she always — less and less frequently of course — trimmed her husband's fluffy wreath of hair with a pair of silver-handled scissors.

She read Meershank's manuscripts with a delicious (to Meershank) frown on her wide pale brow — more and more she'd grown to resemble her mother. She turned over the pages with a delicate hand as though they possessed the same scholarly sheen as her father's *Official History of the Canadian Navy*. She read them not once, but several times, catching a kind of overflow of observance which leaked like oil and vinegar from the edges of Meershank's copious, verbal, many-leafed salads.

Her responses never marched in time with his. She was slower, and could wave aside sentimentality, saying, "Why not? — it's part of the human personality." Occasionally she said the unexpected thing, as when she described her husband's novella, *Fiend at the Water Fountain*, as being, "cool and straight up and down as a tulip."

What she actually told the journalist from *Encounter* was that she never *laughed* when reading her husband's books. For this Meershank has always respected her, valued her, adored her. She was his Canadian rose, his furry imbiber of scented tea, his smiling plum, his bread and jam, his little squirrel, his girlie-girl, his Dear Heart who promised in the garden by the river beside the limestone house in 1949 to stay at his side for ever and ever. What a joke she has played on him in the end.

She has, Meershank said to Maybelle, taken a turn for the worse. He phoned the doctor, who said he would come at once. Then he handed Maybelle a piece of paper on which two telephone numbers were written. "Please," he said. "Phone the children."

Maybelle was unprepared for this. And she had never met the children. "What should I tell them?" she asked.

"Tell them," Meershank said, and paused. "Tell them it could be sooner than we thought."

One of the daughters, Sonya, lived in London, Ontario where she was the new director of the program for women's studies. (For those who trouble to look, her mirror image can be found in Ira Chauvin, post-doc researcher in male studies, in Meershank's academic farce, *Ten Minutes to Tenure*.) Sonya did not say to Maybelle, "Who is this calling?" or "How long does she have?" She said, "I'll be there in three hours flat."

The other daughter, Angelica, ran a health-food restaurant and delicatessen with her husband, Rusty, in Montreal. They were just closing up for the night when Maybelle phoned. "I can get a plane at midnight," Angelica said in a high, sweet, shaky voice. "Tell her to wait for me."

After that Maybelle sat on a kitchen chair in the dark. She could have switched on the light, but she preferred to sit as she was and puzzle over what level of probability had landed her on the twenty-fourth of May as a visitor in a dying woman's shadowy kitchen. And that was what she was, only a visitor — she was not such a fool as to mistake a single embrace for anything other than a mutation of grief.

The tiles of the kitchen wall, after a moment, took on a greenish glow, and she began to float out of her body, a trick she had perfected during her long years of commuting between

Cookston Corners and downtown Toronto. First, she became Sonya flying down an eastbound highway, her hands suddenly younger and supple-jointed on the slippery wheel. She took the long cloverleafs effortlessly, the tires of her tough little car zinging over ramps and bridges, and the sleepy nighttime radio voices holding her steady in the middle lane.

Then, blinking once and shutting out the piny air, she was transformed into Angelica, candid, fearful, sitting tense in an aisle seat at the rear of a plane — she had her mother's smooth cheeks, her father's square chin and her own slow sliding tears. On her lap she clutched a straw bag, and every five minutes she pushed back the sleeve of her blouse and checked her wristwatch, trying to freeze its hands with her will.

Next she was the doctor — springing onto the veranda, tapping at the screen door and taking the stairs two at a time. She drifted then into the amorphous body of Louise where it was hot and damp and difficult to breath, but where shadows reached out and curved around her head. Her hands lay surprisingly calm on the sheet — until one of them was lifted and held to Meershank's beating heart.

She felt his bewilderment and heard with his ears a long popping chain of firecrackers going off. A window in the bedroom had been opened — at last — and the scent of the mock orange blossoms reached him with a rushing blow. Everything was converging. All the warm fluids of life came sliding behind Maybelle's eyes, and she had to hold on to the sides of the kitchen chair to keep herself from disappearing.

In each of Meershank's fictions there is what the literary tribe calls a "set piece," a jewel, as it were, set in a spun-out text, or a chunk of narrative that is somehow more intense, more cohesive, more self-contained than the rest. Generally theatrical and vivid, it can be read and comprehended, even when severed from the wider story, or it can be "performed" by those writers — Meershank is not one — who like to gad about the country giving "readings."

In Meershank's recently published book, *Malaprop in Disney-*

field, the set piece has four characters sitting at dusk on a veranda discussing the final words of the recently deceased family matriarch. The sky they gaze into is a rainy mauve, and the mood is one of tenderness — but there is also a tone of urgency. Three of the four had been present when the last words were uttered, and some irrational prompting makes them want to share with the fourth what they heard — or what they *thought* they heard. Because each heard something different, and there is a descending order of coherence.

"The locked door of the room," is what one of them, a daughter, heard.

"The wok cringes in the womb," is the enigmatic phrase another swears she heard.

The bereaved husband, a blundering old fool in shirtsleeves, heard, incredibly, "The sock is out of tune."

All three witnesses turn to their listener, as lawyers to a judge. Not one of them is superstitious enough to place great importance on final words. Illness, they know, brings a rainbow of distortion, but they long, nevertheless, for interpretation.

The listening judge is an awkward but compassionate woman who would like nothing better than to bring these three fragments into unity. Inside her head she holds a pencil straight up. Her eyes are fixed on the purpling clouds.

Then it arrives. Through some unsecured back door in her imagination she comes up with "The mock orange is in bloom."

"Of course, of course," they chime, nodding and smiling at each other, and at that moment their grief shifts subtly, the first of many such shiftings they are about to undergo.

Pardon

ON FRIDAY AFTERNOON Milly stopped at Ernie's Cards 'n' Things to buy a *mea culpa* card for her father-in-law whom she had apparently insulted.

"Sorry," Ernie's wife said in her testy way. "We're all out."

Milly found this hard to believe. The card rack was full. You could buy a happiness-in-your-new-home card or a mind-your-own-beeswax card, even a spectacular three-dollar pop-up card announcing to the world that you were feeling underappreciated. Surely there was such a thing as an I'm-sorry card.

"You can believe what you want," Ernie's wife said. "But we're sold right out. At the start of the week I had at least a dozen sorry cards in stock. We had a real nice selection, all the way from 'I boobed' to 'Forgive me, Dear Heart.' They went like hotcakes, the whole lot. That's more than I sell in an average year."

"How strange," Milly said. "What on earth's everyone being sorry about all of a sudden?"

Ernie's wife made a gesture of impatience. She wasn't there to stand around jawing with the customers, she snapped. There was the inventory to do and the ordering and so on.

Milly at once apologized for taking up her time; she had only been speaking rhetorically when she asked what everyone was being sorry about.

At this, Ernie's wife had the grace to blush and make amends. She'd been under a strain, she said, what with people in and out of the shop all week grousing about her stock of sorry cards. There was one poor soul who came in weeping her eyes out. She'd had a set-to with her husband and told him he was getting so fat he was no longer attractive to her. It turned out he wasn't really getting fat at all. She was just in a miffy mood because she didn't like the new statue of Louis Riel in the park. She didn't object to Louis in the buff, not that — it was more a question of where her tax dollars were going.

Milly, who was an intimate friend of the sculptor, said, "I'm really sorry to hear this."

"And then," Ernie's wife went on, "a gentleman came in here saying he'd had an out-and-out row with his next-door neighbor who'd been a true-blue friend for twenty years."

"These things happen," Milly said. "Just this week my own father-in-law —"

"Seems this man and his neighbor got on to the subject of politics — in my opinion not a subject for friends to be discussing. This neighbor called my customer a stuffed-shirt fascist right to his face."

"That seems a little extreme," Milly said. "But why should he be the one to send a sorry card when his friend was the one who —?"

"Exactly!" Ernie's wife held up a finger and her eyes filled with fire. "My thoughts exactly. But later that same day who should come in but a sweet old white-haired gent who said his next door neighbor had called him a pinko bleeding heart and he —"

"Do you mean to tell me he was the very —"

"You're interrupting," Ernie's wife cried.

Milly said she was terribly sorry. She explained that she was feeling unstrung because now she would have to go all the way downtown to buy a card for her father-in-law.

"Well, if you're going downtown," Ernie's wife said, "would you mind returning a pair of pajamas for me? I bought them in the sales last week and, lo and behold, I got them home and found a flaw in the left sleeve."

Milly disliked going all the way downtown. She disliked

waiting for the bus, and when she got on the bus she disliked the way a man sitting next to her let his umbrella drip on her ankle.

"I'm most awfully sorry," he said. "I didn't realize. I didn't even notice. In a hundred years I would never have let —"

Milly managed a smile and made a gesture with her hand that said: it's all right, I accept your apology. She was glad the umbrella hadn't dripped on the pajamas Ernie's wife had given her to return. Returning merchandise can be tricky, especially when it's wet and when the receipt's been mislaid. More often than not you meet with suspicion, scorn, arrogance, rebuff.

But today the gentleman in the complaint department was wearing a yellow rose in his lapel and his eyes twinkled.

"We take full responsibility for flaws," he said. "Head office will be sending your friend a letter begging her pardon, and I personally apologize in the name of our branch and in the name of the manufacturer."

Milly, triumphant, took the bus home. The driver apologized, as well he should, for splashing her as she stood at the bus stop.

"It's not your fault, it's all this blessed rain," Milly said.

The bus driver shook his head. "A regular deluge. But I should have been more careful."

The instant the words left his mouth the rain began to fall more heavily. The sky turned an ugly black and soon rain was pelting down, loud and musical, slamming on the roof of the bus and streaming in thick sheets down its sides. The windshield wipers did their best to beat back the water, but clearly they hadn't been designed for a storm of this magnitude and, after a few minutes, the driver pulled over to the curb.

"I'm awfully sorry, folks," he announced, "but we're going to have to wait this one out."

Nobody really minded. It was rather pleasant, almost like a party, to be sitting snugly inside a parked bus whose windows had turned to silver, swapping stories about storms of other years. Several passengers remembered the flood of 1958 and the famous spring downpour of 1972, but most of them agreed that today's storm was the most violent they had ever seen. They would be going home to flooded basements and worried spouses, yet they remained cheerful. Some of the younger people at the back of the bus struck up an impromptu singsong, and the older folks traded their newspapers back and forth. The headline on one paper said TRUDEAU APOLOGIZES TO REAGAN, and another said REAGAN APOLOGIZES TO SUMMIT. By the time the sun burst through, many of the passengers had exchanged names and phone numbers and announced to each other how cleansing a good storm can be, how it sweeps away unspoken hostilities and long-held grudges.

Milly, walking home from her bus stop, breathed in the shining air. Her feet were drenched and she was forced to step over several fallen tree branches, but she noted with pleasure the blue clarity of the sky. It was going to be a splendid evening. A single cloud, a fluffy width of cumulus, floated high in the air over her house. It was shaped like a pair of wings, thought Milly, who was in a fanciful mood. No, not like wings, but like two outstretched hands, wonderfully white and beseeching, which seemed to beckon to her and say: Sorry about all this fuss and bother.

Seeing the great cloudy hands made Milly yearn to absolve all those who had troubled her in her life. She forgave her father for naming her Milly instead of Jo Ann, and her mother for passing on to her genes that made her oversensitive to small hurts and slights. She forgave her brother for reading her diary, and her sister for her pretty legs, and her cat for running in front of a truck and winding up pressed flat as a transfer on the road. She forgave everyone who had ever forgotten her birthday and everyone who looked over her shoulder at parties for someone more attractive to talk to. She forgave her boss for being waspish and her lover for lack of empathy and her husband for making uncalled for remarks about stale breakfast cereal and burned toast.

All this dispensing of absolution emptied Milly out and made her light as air. She had a sensation of floating, of weightlessness, and it seemed to her that bells were chiming inside her head.

But it was only the telephone ringing — without a doubt her father-in-law phoning to ask forgiveness. She hurried inside so she could sing into his ear, yes, yes, yes, yes, yes.

Words

WHEN THE WORLD first started heating up, an international conference was held in Rome to discuss ways of dealing with the situation.

Ian's small northern country — small in terms of population, that is, not in size — sent him to the meetings as a junior observer, and it was there he met Isobel, who was representing her country as a full-fledged delegate. She wore a terrible green dress the first time he saw her, and rather clumsy shoes, but he could see that her neck was slender, her waist narrow and her legs long and brown. For so young a woman, she was astonishingly articulate; in fact, it was her voice more than anything else that he fell in love with — its hills and valleys and its pliant, easy-sided wit. It was a voice that could be distinguished in any gathering, being both sweet and husky and having an edging of contralto merriment that seemed to Ian as rare and fine as a border of gold leaf.

They played truant, missing half the study sessions, the two of them lingering instead over tall, cool drinks in the cafe they found on the Via Traflori. There, under a cheerful striped canopy, Isobel leaned across a little table and placed long, ribbony Spanish phrases into Ian's mouth, encouraging and praising him when he got them right. And he, in his somewhat stiff northern voice, gave back the English equivalents: table, chair, glass, cold, hot, money, street, people, mouth. In the evenings, walking in the gardens in front of the institute where the conference was being held, they turned to each other and promised with their eyes, and in two languages as well, to love each other for ever.

The second International Conference was held ten years later. The situation had become grave. One could use the word *crisis* and not be embarrassed. Ian — by then married to Isobel, who was at home with the children — attended every session, and he listened attentively to the position papers of various physicists, engineers, geographers and linguists from all parts of the world. It was a solemn but distinguished assembly; many eminent men and women took their places at the lectern, including the spidery old Scottish demographer who years earlier had made the first correlation between substrata temperatures and highly verbalized societies. In every case, these speakers presented their concerns with admirable brevity, each word weighted and frugally chosen, and not one of them exceeded the two-minute time limitation. For by now no one really doubted that it was the extravagance and proliferation of language that had caused the temperature of the earth's crust to rise, and in places — California, Japan, London — to crack open and form long ragged lakes of fire. The evidence was everywhere and it was incontrovertible; thermal maps and measurements, sonar readings, caloric separations, a network of subterranean monitoring systems — all these had reinforced the integrity of the original Scottish theories.

But the delegates, sitting in the plenary session of the second International Conference, still were reluctant to take regulatory action. It was partly a case of heads-in-the-sand; it was — human nature being what it is — partly a matter of political advantage or commercial gain. There lingered, too, a somewhat surprising nostalgia for traditional liberties and for the old verbal order of the world. Discussion at the conference had gone around and around all week, pointless and wasteful, and it looked very much as though the final meeting would end in yet another welter of indecision and deferral. It was at that point that Ian, seated in the front row, rose and requested permission to speak.

He was granted a one-minute slot on the agenda. In fact, he spoke for several minutes, but his eloquence, his sincerity (and no doubt his strong, boyish appearance, his shaggy hair and his blue eyes) seemed to merit an exception. Certainly not one person sitting in that gathering had any wish to stop him.

It was unfortunate, tragic some thought, that a freak failure in the electronic system — only a plug accidentally pulled from its socket — prevented his exact words from being recorded, but those who were present remembered afterward how passionately he pleaded his love for the planet. (In truth — though who could know this? — he was thinking chiefly of his love for Isobel and his two children.)

We are living in a fool's dream, he told his fellow delegates, and the time has come for us to wake up. Voluntary restraints were no longer adequate to preserve the little earth, which was the only home we know. Halfway measures like the old three-hour *temps tranquilles* were next to useless since they were never, or almost never, enforced. The evening curfew-lingua was ridiculously lenient. Abuses of every sort abounded, particularly the use of highly percussive words or words that were redolent with emotional potency, even though it had been established that these two classes of words were particularly damaging to bedrock and shales. Multilingualism continued to flourish. Wasteful antiphonic structures were actually on the increase in the more heavily populated regions, as was the use of elaborate ceremonial metaphor. It was as though, by refusing to make linguistic sacrifices, the human race had willed its own destruction.

When he finished speaking, the applause was prolonged and powerful. It perhaps held an element of shame, too; this young man had found the courage to say at last what should have been said long before. One after another the delegates rose to their feet, and soon their clapping fell into a steady rhythmic beat which had the effect of holding Ian hostage on the platform. The chairman whispered into his ear, begging him for a few additional words.

He assented. He could not say no. And, in a fever that was remarkably similar to the fever he had suffered as a child during a severe case of measles, or like the fever of love he had succumbed to ten years earlier in Rome, he announced to the audience, holding up a hand for attention, that he would be the first to take a vow of complete silence for the sake of the planet that had fathered him.

Almost at once he regretted his words, but hubris kept him from recanting for the first twenty-four hours and, after that, a kind of stubbornness took over. Isobel met him at the airport with the words, "You went too far." Later, after a miserable, silent attempt at lovemaking, she said, "I'll never forgive you." His children, clamoring to hear about his moment of heroism, poked at him, at his face and chest and arms, as though he were inert. He tried to tell them with his eyes that he was still their father, that he still loved them.

"Leave him alone," Isobel said sharply. "He might as well be a stranger now. He's no different than anyone else."

She became loud and shrewish. When his silent followers arrived at their door — and in time there were thousands of them, each with the same blank face and gold armband — she admitted them with bad grace. She grew garrulous. She rambled on and on, bitter and blaming, sometimes incoherent, sometimes obscene, sometimes reverting to a coarse, primitive schoolyard Spanish, sometimes shouting to herself or cursing into the mirror or chanting oaths — anything to furnish the emptiness of the house with words. She became disoriented. The solid plaster of the walls fell away from her, melting into a drift of vapor. There seemed to be no shadows, no sense of dimension, no delicate separation between one object and another. Privately she pleaded with her husband for an act of apostasy. Later she taunted him. "Show me you're still human," she would say. "Give me just one word." The word *betrayal* came frequently out of her wide mobile mouth, and so did the scornful epithet *martyr*.

But time passes and people forget. She forgot, finally, what it was that had betrayed her. Next she forgot her husband's name. Sometimes she forgot that she had a husband at all, for how could anything be said to exist, she asked herself loudly, hoarsely — even a husband, even one's self — if it didn't also exist in the shape of a word.

He worried that she might be arrested, but for some reason, his position probably, she was always let off with a warning. In their own house she ignored him, passing him on the stairs without a look, or crossing in front of him as though he were a stuffed chair. Often she disappeared for hours, venturing out alone into the heat of the night, and he began to suspect she had taken a lover.

The thought preyed on him, though in fact he had long since forgotten the word for *wife* and also the word for *fidelity*. One night, when she left the house, he attempted to follow her, but clearly she was suspicious because she walked very quickly, looking back over her shoulder, making a series of unnecessary turns and choosing narrow old streets whose curbs were blackened by fire. Within minutes he lost sight of her; soon after that he was driven back by the heat.

The next night he tried again, and this time he saw her disappear into an ancient, dilapidated building, the sort of enclosure, he remembered, where children had once gone to learn to read and write. Unexpectedly he felt a flash of pity; what a sad place for a tryst. He waited briefly, then entered the building and went up a flight of smoldering stairs which seemed on the point of collapse. There he found a dim corridor, thick with smoke, and a single room at one end.

Through the door he heard a waterfall of voices. There must have been a dozen people inside, all of them talking. The talk seemed to be about poetry. Someone — a woman — was giving a lecture. There were interruptions, a discussion, some laughter. He heard his wife's voice, her old gilt-edged contralto, asking a question, and the sound of it made him draw in his breath so sharply that something hard, like a cinder or a particle of gravel, formed in his throat.

It stayed stubbornly lodged there all night. He found it painful to breath, and even Isobel noticed how he thrashed about in bed, gasping wildly for air. In the morning she called a doctor, who could find nothing wrong, but she remained uneasy, and that evening she stayed home and made him cups of iced honey-and-lemon tea to ease his throat. He took her hand at one point and held it to his lips as though it might be possible to find the air he needed inside the crevices of her skin. By now the scraping in his throat had become terrible, a raw agonizing rasp like a dull knife sawing through limestone. She looked at his face from which the healthy, blood-filled elasticity had gone out and felt herself brushed by a current of air or what might have been the memory of a name.

He began to choke violently, and she heard something grotesque come out of his mouth, a sound that was only half-human, but which rode on a curious rhythmic wave that for some reason stirred her deeply. She imagined it to be the word *Isobel*. "Isobel?" she asked, trying to remember its meaning. He said it a second time, and this time the syllables were more clearly formed.

The light of terror came into his eyes, or perhaps the beginning of a new fever; she managed to calm him by stroking his arm. Then she called the children inside the house, locked the doors and windows against the unbearable heat, and they began, hands linked, at the beginning where they had begun before — with table, chair, bed, cool, else, other, sleep, face, mouth, breath, tongue.

Slowly, patiently.

Poaching

ON OUR WAY to catch the Portsmouth ferry, Dobey and I stayed overnight at a country hotel in the village of Kingsclere. The floors sloped, the walls tipped, the tap leaked rusty water and the bedclothes gave out an old, bitter odor.

At breakfast we were told by the innkeeper that King John had once stayed in this hotel and, moreover, had slept in the very room where we had spent the night.

"Wasn't he the Magna Carta king?" Dobey said, showing off. "That would make it early thirteenth century."

"Incredible," I said, worrying whether I should conceal my fried bread beneath the underdone bacon or the bacon beneath the bread. "Extraordinary."

The innkeeper had more to tell us. "And when His Royal Highness stopped here he was bit by a bedbug. Of course there's none of that nowadays." Here he chuckled a hearty chuckle and sucked in his red cheeks.

I crushed my napkin — Dobey would call it a serviette — on top of my bacon and fried bread and egg yolk and said to myself: next he'll be rattling on about a ghost.

"And I didn't like to tell you people last night when you arrived," the innkeeper continued, "but the room where the two of you was — it's haunted."

"King John?" I asked.

"One of the guards, it's thought. My wife's seen 'im many the time. And our Barbara. And I've heard 'im clomping about in his great boots in the dark of the night and making a right awful noise."

Dobey and I went back to our room to brush our teeth and

close our haversacks, and then we lay flat on our backs for a minute on the musty bed and stared at the crooked beams.

"Are you thinking kingly thoughts?" I said after a while.

"I'm thinking about those poor bloody Aussies," said Dobey.

"Oh, them," I said. "They'll make out all right."

Only the day before we'd picked up the two Australians on the road. Not that they were by any stretch your average hitchhikers — two women, a mother, middle-aged, and a grown daughter, both smartly dressed. Their rented Morris Minor had started to smoke between Farrington and Kingsclere, and we gave them a lift into the village.

They'd looked us over carefully, especially the mother, before climbing into the backseat. We try to keep the backseat clean and free of luggage for our hitchhikers. The trick is to put them at their ease so they'll talk. Some we wring dry just by keeping quiet. For others we have to prime the pump. It's like stealing, Dobey says, only no one's thought to make a law against it.

Within minutes we knew all about the Australians. They were from Melbourne. The mother had recently been widowed, and her deceased husband, before the onset of Addison's disease, had worked as an investment analyst. Something coppery about the way she said "my late husband" suggested marital dullness, but Dobey and I never venture into inter-pretation. The daughter taught in a junior school. She was engaged to be married, a chap in the military. The wedding was six months away, and the two of them, mother and daughter, were shoring themselves up by spending eight weeks touring Britain, a last fling before buckling down to wedding arrange-ments. It was to be a church ceremony followed by a lobster lunch in the ballroom of a large hotel.

The two of them made the wedding plans sound grudging and complex and tiresome, like putting on a war. The daughter emitted a sigh; nothing ever went right. And now they'd only been in England a week, had hardly made a dent, and already the hired car had let them down. It looked serious, too, maybe the clutch.

Everything the mother said seemed electrically amplified by

her bright, forthcoming Australia-laquered voice. She had an optimistic nature, quickly putting the car out of mind and chirping away from the back seat about the relations in Exeter they planned to visit, elderly aunts, crippled uncles, a nephew who'd joined a rock band and traveled to America, was signed up by a movie studio but never was paid a penny — all this we learned in the ten minutes it took us to drive them into Kingsclere and drop them at the phone box. The daughter, a pretty girl with straight blond hair tied back in a ribbon, hardly said a word.

Nor did we. Dobey and I had made a pact at the start of the trip that we would conceal ourselves, our professions, our antecedents, where we lived, what we were to each other. We would dwindle, grow deliberately thin, almost invisible, and live like aerial plants off the packed fragments and fictions of the hitchhikers we picked up.

One day we traveled for two hours — this was between Conway and Manchester — with a lisping, blue-jeaned giant from Canada who'd come to England to write a doctoral thesis on the early language theories of Wittgenstein.

"We owe tho muth to Withgenstein," he sputtered, sweeping a friendly red paw through the air and including Dobey and me in the circle of Wittgenstein appreciators. He had run out of money. First he sold his camera; then his Yamaha recorder; then, illegally, the British Rail Pass his parents had given him when he finished his master's degree. That was why he was hitchhiking. He said, "I am going to Oxthford" as though he was saying, "I am a man in love."

He talked rapidly, not at all embarassed by his lisp — Dobey and I liked him for that, though normally we refrain from forming personal judgments about our passengers. He spoke as though compelled to explain to us his exact reason for being where he was at that moment.

They all do. It is a depressing hypothesis, but probably, as Dobey says, true: people care only about themselves. They are frenzied and driven, but only by the machinery of their own adventuring. It has been several days now since anyone's asked us who we are and what we're doing driving around like this.

Usually Dobey drives, eyes on the road, listening with a supple, restless attention. I sit in the front passenger seat, my brain screwed up in a squint from looking sideways. At times I feel that giving lifts to strangers makes us into patronizing benefactors. But Dobey says this is foolish; these strangers buy their rides with their stories.

Dobey prefers to pick up strangers who are slightly distraught, saying they "unwind" more easily. Penury or a burned-out clutch — these work in our favor and save us from having to frame our careful questions. I am partial, though, to the calm, to those who stand by the roadside with their luggage in the dust, too composed or dignified to trouble the air with their thumbs. There was that remarkable Venezuelan woman who rode with us from Cardiff to Conway and spoke only inter-mittently and in sentences that seemed wrapped in their own cool vapors. Yes, she adored to travel alone. She liked the song of her own thoughts. She was made fat by the sight of mountains. The Welsh sky was blue like a cushion. She was eager to embrace rides from strangers. She liked to open wide windows so she could commune with the wind. She was a doctor, a specialist in bones, but alas, alas, she was not in love with her profession. She was in love with the English language because every word could be picked up and spun like a coin on the table top.

The shyest traveler can be kindled, Dobey maintains — often after just one or two strikes of the flint. That sullen Lancashire girl with the pink-striped hair and the colloid eyes — her dad was a coward, her mum shouted all the time, her boyfriend had broken her nose and got her pregnant. She was on her way, she told us, to a hostel in Bolton. Someone there would help her out. She had the address written on the inside of a cigarette packet. I looked aslant and could tell that Dobey wanted to offer her money, but part of our bargain was that we offer only rides.

Another thing we agreed on was that we would believe everything we were told. No matter how fantastic or eccentric or crazy the stories we heard, we'd pledged ourselves to respect their surfaces. Anyone who stepped into our backseat was trusted, even the bearded, evil-smelling curmudgeon we picked up in Sheffield who told us that the spirit of Ben Jonson had directed him to go to Westminster and stand at the abbey door preaching obedience to Mrs. Thatcher. We not only humored the old boy — who gave us shaggy, hand-rolled cigarettes to smoke — but we delivered him at midnight that same day.

Nevertheless, I'm becoming disillusioned. (It was my idea to head for Portsmouth and cross the channel.) I long, for instance, to let slip to one of our passengers that Dobey and I have slept in the bedchamber where King John was nipped by a bedbug. It's not attention I want and certainly not admiration. It's only that I'd like to float my own story on the air. I want to test its buoyancy, to see if it holds any substance, to see if it's true or the opposite of true.

And I ask myself about the stories we've been hearing lately: have they grown thinner? The Australian mother and daughter, for example — what had they offered? Relations in Exeter. A wedding in Melbourne. Is that enough? Dobey says to be patient, that everything is fragmentary, that it's up to us to supply the missing links. Behind each of the people we pick up, Dobey believes, there's a deep cave, and in the cave is a trap door and a set of stone steps which we may descend if we wish. I say to Dobey that there may be nothing at the bottom of the stairs, but Dobey says, how will we know if we don't look.

Scenes

IN 1974 FRANCES was asked to give a lecture in Edmonton, and on the way there her plane was forced to make an emergency landing in a barley field. The man sitting next to her — they had not spoken — turned and asked if he might put his arms around her. She assented. They clung together, her size 12 dress and his wool suit. Later, he gave her his business card.

She kept the card for several weeks poked in the edge of her bedroom mirror. It is a beautiful mirror, a graceful rectangle in a pine frame, and very, very old. Once it was attached to the back of a bureau belonging to Frances' grandmother. Leaves, vines, flowers and fruit are shallowly carved in the soft wood of the frame. The carving might be described as primitive — and this is exactly why Frances loves it, being drawn to those things that are incomplete or in some way flawed. Furthermore, the mirror is the first thing she remembers seeing, *really* seeing, as a child. Visiting her grandmother, she noticed the stiff waves of light and shadow on the frame, the way square pansies interlocked with rigid grapes, and she remembers creeping out of her grandmother's bed where she had been put for an afternoon nap and climbing on a chair so she could touch the worked surface with the flat of her hand.

Her grandmother died. It was discovered by the aunts and uncles that on the back of the mirror was stuck a piece of adhesive tape and on the tape was written: "For my vain little granddaughter Frances." Frances' mother was affronted, but put it down to hardening of the arteries. Frances, who was only seven, felt uniquely, mysteriously honored.

She did not attend the funeral; it was thought she was too young, and so instead she was taken one evening to the funeral home to bid goodbye to her grandmother's body. The room where the old lady lay was large, quiet, and hung all around with swags of velvet. Frances' father lifted her up so she could see her grandmother, who was wearing a black dress with a white crepe jabot, her powdered face pulled tight as though with a drawstring into a sort of grimace. A lovely blanket with satin edging covered her trunky legs and torso. Laid out, calm and silent as a boat, she looked almost generous.

For some reason Frances was left alone with the casket for a few minutes, and she took this chance — she had to pull herself up on tiptoe — to reach out and touch her grandmother's lips with the middle finger of her right hand. It was like pressing in the side of a rubber ball. The lips did not turn to dust — which did not surprise Frances at all, but rather confirmed what she had known all along. Later, she would look at her finger and say to herself, "This finger has touched dead lips." Then she would feel herself grow rich with disgust. The touch, she knew, had not been an act of love at all, but only a kind of test.

With the same middle finger she later touched the gelatinous top of a goldfish swimming in a little glass bowl at school. She touched the raised mole on the back of her father's white neck. Shuddering, she touched horse turds in the back lane, and she touched her own urine springing onto the grass as she squatted behind the snowball bush by the fence. When she looked into her grandmother's mirror, now mounted on her own bedroom wall, she could hardly believe that she, Frances, had contravened so many natural laws.

The glass itself was beveled all the way around, and she can remember that she took pleasure in lining up her round face so that the beveled edge split it precisely in two. When she was fourteen she wrote in her diary, "Life is like looking into a beveled mirror." The next day she crossed it out and, peering into the mirror, stuck out her tongue and made a face. All her life she'd had this weakness for preciosity, but mainly she'd managed to keep it in check.

She is a lithe and toothy woman with strong, thick, dark-brown hair, now starting to gray. She can be charming. "Frances can charm the bees out of the hive," said a friend of hers, a man she briefly thought she loved. Next year she'll be forty-five — terrible! — but at least she's kept her figure. A western sway to her voice is what people chiefly remember about her, just as they remember other people for their chins or noses. This voice sometimes makes her appear inquisitive, but, in fact, she generally hangs back and leaves it to others to begin a conversation.

Once, a woman got into an elevator with her and said, "Will you forgive me if I speak my mind. This morning I came within an inch of taking my life. There was no real reason, only everything had got suddenly so dull. But I'm all right now. In fact, I'm going straight to a restaurant and treat myself to a plate of french fries. Just fries, not even a sandwich to go with them. I was never allowed to have french fries when I was a little girl, but the time comes when a person should do what she wants to do."

The subject of childhood interests Frances, especially its prohibitions, so illogical and various, and its random doors and windows which appear solidly shut, but can, in fact, be opened easily with a touch or a password or a minute of devout resolution. It helps to be sly, also to be quick. There was a time when she worried that fate had penciled her in as "debilitated by guilt," but mostly she takes guilt for what it is, a kind of lover who can be shrugged off or greeted at the gate. She looks at her two daughters and wonders if they'll look back resentfully, recalling only easy freedoms and an absence of terror — in other words, meagerness — and envy her for her own stern beginnings. It turned out to have been money in the bank, all the various shames and sweats of growing up. It was instructive; it kept things interesting; she still shivers, remembering how exquisitely sad she was as a child.

"It's only natural for children to be sad," says her husband, Theo, who, if he has a fault, is given to reductive statements. "Children are unhappy because they are inarticulate and hence lonely."

Frances can't remember being lonely, but telling this to Theo is like blowing into a hurricane. She was spoiled — a lovely word, she thinks — and adored by her parents, her plump, white-faced father and her skinny, sweet-tempered mother. Their love was immense and enveloping like a fall of snow. In the evenings, winter evenings, she sat between the two of them on a blue nubby sofa, listening to the varnished radio and taking sips from their cups of tea from time to time or sucking on a spoonful of sugar. The three of them sat enthralled through "Henry Aldrich" and "Fibber Magee and Molly," and when Frances laughed they looked at her and laughed too. Frances has no doubt that those spoonfuls of sugar and the roar of Fibber Magee's closet and her parents' soft looks were taken in and preserved so that she, years later, boiling an egg or making love or digging in the garden, is sometimes struck by a blow of sweetness that seems to come out of nowhere.

The little brown house where she grew up sat in the middle of a block crowded with other such houses. In front of each lay a tiny lawn and a flower bed edged with stones. Rows of civic trees failed to flourish, but did not die either. True, there was terror in the back lane where the big boys played with sticks and jackknives, but the street was occupied mainly by quiet, hard-working families, and in the summertime hopscotch could be played in the street, there was so little traffic.

Frances' father spent his days "at the office." Her mother stayed at home, wore bib aprons, made jam and pickles and baked custard, and every morning before school brushed and braided Frances' hair. Frances can remember, or thinks she can remember, that one morning her mother walked as far as the corner with her and said, "I don't know why, but I'm so full of happiness today I can hardly bear it." The sun came fretting through the branches of a scrubby elm at that minute and splashed across her mother's face, making her look like someone in a painting or like one of the mothers in her school reader.

Learning to read was like falling into a mystery deeper than the mystery of airwaves or the halo around the head of the baby Jesus. Deliberately she made herself stumble and falter over the words in her first books, trying to hold back the rush of revelation. She saw other children being matter-of-fact and methodical, puzzling over vowels and consonants and sounding out words as though they were dimes and nickels that had to be extracted from the slot of a bank. She felt suffused with light and often skipped or hopped or ran wildly to keep herself from flying apart.

Her delirium, her failure to ingest books calmly, made her suspect there was something wrong with her or else with the world, yet she deeply distrusted the school librarian who insisted that a book could be a person's best friend. (Those subject to preciosity instantly spot others with the same affliction.) This librarian, Miss Mayes, visited all the classes. She was tall and soldierly with a high, light voice. "Boys and girls," she cried, bringing large red hands together, "a good book will never let you down." She went on; books could take you on magic journeys; books could teach you where the rain came from or how things used to be in the olden days. A person who truly loved books need never feel alone.

But, she continued, holding up a finger, there are people who do shameful things to books. They pull them from the shelves by their spines. They turn down the corners of pages; they leave them on screened porches where the rain and other elements can warp their covers; and they use curious and inappropriate objects as bookmarks.

From a petit-point bag she drew a list of objects that had been wrongly, criminally inserted between fresh clean pages: a blue-jay feather, an oak leaf, a matchbook cover, a piece of colored chalk and, on one occasion — "on one occasion, boys and girls" — a *strip of bacon*.

A strip of bacon. In Frances' mind the strip of bacon was uncooked, cold and fatty with a pathetic streaking of lean. Its oil would press into the paper, a porky abomination, and its ends would flop out obscenely. The thought was thrilling: someone, someone who lived in the same school district, had had the audacity, the imagination, to mark the pages of a book with a strip of bacon. The existence of this person and his outrageous act penetrated the fever that had come over her since she'd learned to read, and she began to look around again and see what the world had to offer.

Next door lived Mr. and Mrs. Shaw, and upstairs, fast asleep, lived Louise Shaw, aged eighteen. She had been asleep for ten years. A boy across the street named Jackie McConnell told Frances that it was the sleeping sickness, that Louise Shaw had been bitten by the sleeping sickness bug, but Frances' mother said no, it was the coma. One day Mrs. Shaw, smelling of chlorine bleach and wearing a flower-strewn housedress, stopped Frances on the sidewalk, held the back of her hand to the side of Frances' face and said, "Louise was just your age when we lost her. She was forever running or skipping rope or throwing a ball up against the side of the garage. I used to say to her, don't make such a ruckus, you'll drive me crazy. I used to yell all the time at her, she was so full of beans and such a chatterbox." After that Frances felt herself under an obligation to Mrs. Shaw, and whenever she saw her she made her body speed up and whirl on the grass or do cartwheels.

A little later she learned to negotiate the back lane. There, between board fences, garbage cans, garage doors and stands of tough weeds, she became newly nimble and strong. She learned to swear — damn, hell and dirty bastard — and played piggy-move-up and spud and got herself roughly kissed a number of times, and then something else happened: one of the neighbors put up a basketball hoop. For a year, maybe two — Frances doesn't trust her memory when it comes to time — she was obsessed with doing free throws. She became known as the queen of free throws; she acquired status, even with the big boys, able to sink ten out of ten baskets, but never, to her sorrow, twenty out of twenty. She threw free throws in the morning before school, at lunchtime, and in the evening until it got dark. Nothing made her happier than when the ball dropped silently through the ring without touching it or banking on the board. At night she dreamed of these silky baskets, the rush of air and the sinuous movement of the net, then the ball striking the pavement and returning to her hands.

("Sounds a bit Freudian to me," her husband, Theo, said when she tried to describe for him her time of free-throw madness, proving once again how far apart the two of them were in some things.) One morning she was up especially early. There was no one about. The milkman hadn't yet come, and there was dew shining on the tarry joints of the pavement. Holding the ball in her hands was like holding onto a face, it was so dearly familiar with its smell of leather and its seams and laces. That morning she threw twenty-seven perfect free throws before missing. Each time the ball went through the hoop she felt an additional oval of surprise grow round her body. She had springs inside her, in her arms and in the insteps of her feet. What stopped her finally was her mother calling her name, demanding to know what she was doing outside so early. "Nothing," Frances said, and knew for the first time the incalculable reward of self-possession.

There was a girl in her sewing class named Pat Leonard. She was older than the other girls, had a rough pitted face and a brain pocked with grotesqueries. "Imagine," she said to Frances, "sliding down a banister and suddenly it turns into a razor blade." When she trimmed the seams of the skirt she was making and accidentally cut through the fabric, she laughed out loud. To amuse the other girls she sewed the skin of her fingers together. She told a joke, a long story about a pickle factory that was really about eating excrement. In her purse was a packet of cigarettes. She had a boyfriend who went to the technical school, and several times she'd reached inside his pants and squeezed his thing until it went off like a squirt gun. She'd flunked math twice. She could hardly read. One day she wasn't there, and the sewing teacher said she'd been expelled. Frances felt as though she'd lost her best friend, even though she wouldn't have been seen dead walking down the hall with Pat Leonard. Melodramatic tears swam into her eyes, and then real tears that wouldn't stop until the teacher brought her a glass of water and offered to phone her mother.

Another time, she was walking home from a friend's in the early evening. She passed by a little house not far from her own. The windows were open and, floating on the summer air, came the sound of people speaking in a foreign language. There seemed to be a great number of them, and the conversation was very rapid and excited. They might have been quarreling or telling old stories; Frances had no idea which. It could have been French or Russian or Portuguese they spoke. The words ran together and made queer little dashes and runs and choking sounds. Frances imagined immense, wide-branching grammars and steep, stone streets rising out of other centuries. She felt as though she'd been struck by a bolt of good fortune, and all because the world was bigger than she'd been led to believe.

At university, where she studied languages, she earned pocket money by working in the library. She and a girl named Ursula were entrusted with the key, and it was their job to open the library on Saturday mornings. During the minute or two before anyone else came, the two of them galloped at top speed through the reference room, the periodical room, the reading room, up and down the rows of stacks, filling that stilled air with what could only be called primal screams. Why this should have given Frances such exquisite pleasure she couldn't have said, since she was in rebellion against nothing she knew of. By the time the first students arrived, she and Ursula would be standing behind the main desk, date stamp in hand, sweet as dimity.

One Saturday, the first person who came was a bushy-headed, serious-minded zoology student named Theodore, called Theo by his friends. He gave Frances a funny look, then in a cracked, raspy voice asked her to come with him later and have a cup of coffee. A year later he asked her to marry him. He had a mind unblown by self-regard and lived, it seemed to Frances, in a nursery world of goodness and badness with not much room to move in between.

It's been mainly a happy marriage. Between the two of them, they've invented hundreds of complex ways of enslaving each other, some of them amazingly tender. Like other married people, they've learned to read each other's minds. Once Theo said to Frances as they drove around and around, utterly lost in a vast treeless suburb, "In every one of these houses there's been a declaration of love," and this was exactly the thought Frances had been thinking.

She has been faithful. To her surprise, to everyone's surprise, she turned out to have an aptitude for monogamy. Nevertheless, many of the scenes that have come into her life have involved men. Once she was walking down a very ordinary French street on a hot day. A man, bare-chested, drinking Perrier at a café table, sang out, *"Bonjour."* Not *"Bonjour, madame"* or *"Bonjour, mademoiselle,"* just *"Bonjour."* Cheeky. She was wearing white pants, a red blouse, a straw hat and sunglasses. *"Bonjour,"* she sang back and gave a sassy little kick, which became the start of a kind of dance. The man at the table clapped his hands over his head to keep time as she went dancing by.

Once she went to the British Museum to finish a piece of research. There was a bomb alert just as she entered, and everyone's shopping bags and briefcases were confiscated and searched. It happened that Frances had just bought a teddy bear for the child of a friend she was going to visit later in the day. The guard took it, shook it till its eyes rolled, and then carried it away to be X-rayed. Later he brought it to Frances, who was sitting at a table examining a beautiful old manuscript. As he handed her the bear, he kissed the air above its fuzzy head, and Frances felt her mouth go into the shape of a kiss, too, a kiss she intended to be an expression of her innocence, only that. He winked. She winked back. He leaned over and whispered into her ear a suggestion that was hideously, comically, obscene. She pretended not to hear, and a few minutes later she left, hurrying down the street full of cheerful shame, her work unfinished.

These are just some of the scenes in Frances' life. She thinks of them as scenes because they're much too fragmentary to be stories and far too immediate to be memories. They seem to bloom out of nothing, out of the thin, uncolored air of defeats and pleasures. A curtain opens, a light appears, there are voices or music or sometimes a wide transparent stream of silence.

Only rarely do they point to anything but themselves. They're difficult to talk about. They're useless, attached to nothing, can't be traded in or shaped into instruments to prise open the meaning of the universe.

There are people who think such scenes are ornaments suspended from lives that are otherwise busy and useful. Frances knows perfectly well that they are what a life is made of, one fitting against the next like English paving-stones.

Or sometimes she thinks of them as little keys on a chain, keys that open nothing, but simply exist for the beauty of their toothed edges and the way they chime in her pocket.

Other times she is reminded of the Easter eggs her mother used to bring out every year. These were real hens' eggs with a hole poked in the top and bottom and the contents blown out. The day before Easter, Frances and her mother always sat down at the kitchen table with paint brushes, a glass of water and a box of watercolors. They would decorate half-a-dozen eggs, maybe more, but only the best were saved from year to year. These were taken from a cupboard just before Easter, removed from their shoebox, and carefully arranged, always on the same little pewter cake stand. The eggs had to be handled gently, especially the older ones.

Frances, when she was young, liked to pick up each one in turn and examine it minutely. She had a way of concentrating her thoughts and shutting everything else out, thinking only of this one little thing, this little egg that was round like the world, beautiful in color and satin to the touch, and that fit into the hollow of her hand as though it were made for that very purpose.

Fragility

WE ARE FLYING over the Rockies on our way to Vancouver, and there sits Ivy with her paperback. I ask myself: should I interrupt and draw her attention to the grandeur beneath us?

In a purely selfish sense, watching Ivy read is as interesting as peering down at those snowy mountains. She turns the pages of a book in the same way she handles every object, with a peculiar respectful gentleness, as though the air around it were more tender than ordinary air. I've watched her lift a cup of tea with this same abstracted grace, cradling a thick mug in a way that transforms it into something precious and fragile. It's a gift some people have.

I decide not to disturb her; utterly absorbed in what she's reading, she's seen the Rockies before.

In the seat ahead of us is a young man wearing a bright blue jacket — I remember that once I had a similar jacket in a similar hue. Unlike us, he's clearly flying over the Rockies for the first time. He's in a half-standing position at the window, snapping away with his camera, pausing only to change the film. From where I'm sitting I can see his intense, eager trigger hand, his steadying elbow, his dropped lower lip. In a week he'll be passing his slides around the office, holding them delicately at their edges up to the light. He might set up a projector and screen them one evening in his living room; he might invite a few friends over, and his wife — who will resemble the Ivy of fifteen years ago — will serve coffee and wedges of cheese cake; these are the Rockies, he'll say — magnificent, stirring, one of the wonders of the continent.

I tell myself that I would give a great deal to be in that young man's shoes, but this is only a half-truth, the kind of lie Ivy and I sometimes spin for our own amusement. We really don't want to go back in time. What we envy in the young is that fine nervous edge of perception, the ability to take in reality afresh. I suppose, as we grow older, that's what we forfeit, acquiring in its place a measure of healthy resignation.

Ivy puts down her book suddenly and reaches for my hand. A cool, light, lazy touch. She's smiling.

"Good book?"

"Hmmm," she says, and stretches.

Now, as a kind of duty, I point out the Rockies.

"Beautiful," she exclaims, leaning toward the window.

And it *is* beautiful. But unfortunately the plane is flying at a height that extracts all sense of dimension from the view. Instead of snow-capped splendor, we see a kind of Jackson-Pollock dribbling of white on green. It's a vast abstract design, a linking of incised patterns, quite interesting in its way, but without any real suggestion of height or majesty.

"It looks a little like a Jackson Pollock," Ivy says in that rhythmic voice of hers.

"Did you really say that?"

"I think so." Her eyebrows go up, her mouth crimps at the edges. "At least, if I didn't, someone did."

I lift her hand — I can't help myself — and kiss her fingertips.

"And what's that for?" she asks, still smiling.

"An attack of poignancy."

"A serious new dietary disease, I suppose," Ivy says, and at that moment the steward arrives with our lunch trays.

Ivy and I have been to Vancouver fairly often on business trips or for holidays. This time it's different; in three months we'll be moving permanently to Vancouver, and now the two of us are engaged in that common-enough errand, a house-hunting expedition.

Common, I say, but not for us.

We know the statistics: that about half of all North Americans move every five years, that we're a rootless, restless, portable society. But for some reason, some failing on our part or perhaps simple good fortune, Ivy and I seem to have evaded the statistical pattern. The small stone-fronted, bow-windowed house we bought when Christopher was born is the house in which we continue to live after twenty years.

If there had been another baby, we would have considered a move, but we stayed in the same house in the middle of Toronto. It was close to both our offices and close too to the clinic Christopher needed. Curiously enough, most of our neighbors also stayed there year after year. In our neighborhood we know everyone. When the news of my transfer came, the first thing Ivy said was, "What about the Mattisons and the Levensons? What about Robin and Sara?"

"We can't very well take everyone on the street along with us."

"Oh Lordy," Ivy said and bit her lip. "Of course not. It's only —"

"I know," I said.

"Maybe we can talk Robin and Sara into taking their holidays on the coast next year. Sara always said —"

"And we'll be back fairly often. At least twice a year."

"If only —"

"If only what?"

"Those stupid bulbs." (I love the way Ivy pronounces the word stupid: *stewpid*, giving it a patrician lift.)

"Bulbs?"

"Remember last fall, all those bulbs I put in?"

"Oh," I said, remembering.

She looked at me squarely: "You don't mind as much as I do, do you?"

"Of course I do. You know I do."

"Tell me the truth."

What could I say? I've always been impressed by the accuracy of Ivy's observations. "The truth is—"

"The truth is —?" she helped me along.

"I guess I'm ready."

"Ready for what?" Her eyes filled with tears. This was a difficult time for us. Christopher had died in January. He was a tough kid and lived a good five years longer than any of us ever thought he would. His death was not unexpected, but still, Ivy and I were feeling exceptionally fragile.

"Ready for what?" she asked again.

"For something," I admitted. "For anything, I guess."

The first house we look at seems perfect. The settled neighborhood is dense with trees and shrubbery and reminds us both of our part of Toronto. There are small repairs that need doing, but nothing major. Best of all, from the dining room there can be seen a startling lip of blue water meeting blue sky.

I point this out to Ivy; a view was one of the things we had put on our list. There is also a fireplace, another must, and a capacious kitchen with greenhouse windows overlooking a garden.

"And look at the bulbs," I point out. "Tulips halfway up. Daffodils."

"Lilies," Ivy says.

"I think we've struck it lucky," I tell the real-estate woman who's showing us around, a Mrs. Marjorie Little. ("Call me Marge," she'd said to us with west-coast breeziness.)

Afterwards, in the car, Ivy is so quiet I have to prompt her. "Well?"

Marge Little, sitting at the wheel, peers at me, then at Ivy.

"It's just," Ivy begins, "it's just so depressing."

Depressing? I can't believe she's saying this. A view, central location, a fireplace. Plus bulbs.

"Well," Ivy says slowly, "it's a divorce house. You must have noticed?"

I hadn't. "A divorce house? How do you know?"

"I looked in the closets. Her clothes were there but *his* weren't."

"Oh."

"And half the pictures had been taken off the wall. Surely you noticed that."

I shake my head.

"I know it sounds silly, but wouldn't you rather move into a house with some good" — she pauses — "some good vibrations?"

"Vibrations?"

"Did you notice the broken light in the bathroom? I'll bet someone threw something at it. In a rage."

"We could always fix the light. And the other things. And with our own furniture — "

Ivy is an accountant. Once I heard a young man in her firm describe her as a *crack* accountant. For a number of years now she's been a senior partner. When this same young man heard she was leaving because of my transfer, he couldn't help ragging her a little, saying he thought women didn't move around at the whim of their husbands anymore, and that, out of principle, she ought to refuse to go to Vancouver or else arrange some kind of compromise life — separate apartments, for instance, with weekend rendezvous in Winnipeg.

Ivy had howled at this. She's a positive, good-natured woman and, as it turned out, she had no trouble finding an opening in a good Vancouver firm at senior level. As I say, she's positive. Which is why her apprehension over good or bad vibrations is puzzling. Can it be she sees bad times ahead for the two of us? Or is it only that she wants solid footing after these long years with Christopher? Neither of us is quite glued back together again. Not that we ever will be.

"I can't help it," Ivy is saying. "It just doesn't feel like a lucky house. There's something about — "

Marge Little interrupts with a broad smile. "I've got all kinds of interesting houses to show you. Maybe you'll like the next one better."

"Does it have good vibes?" Ivy asks, laughing a little to show she's only half-serious.

"I don't know," Marge Little says. "They don't put that kind of info on the fact sheet."

The next house is perched on the side of the canyon. No, that's not quite true. It is, in fact, falling into the canyon. I notice, but don't mention, the fact that the outside foundation walls are cracked and patched. Inside, the house is alarmingly empty; the cool settled air seems proof that it's been vacant for some time.

Marge consults her fact sheet. Yes, the house has been on the market about six months. The price has been reduced twice. But — she glances at us — perhaps we noticed the foundation....

"Yes," I say. "Hopeless."

"Damn," Ivy says.

We look at two more houses; both have spectacular views and architectural distinction. But one is a bankruptcy sale and the other is a divorce house. By now I'm starting to pick up the scent: it's a compound of petty carelessness and strenuous neglect, as though the owners had decamped in a hurry, angry at the rooms themselves.

To cheer ourselves up, the three of us have lunch in a sunny Broadway restaurant. It seems extraordinary that we can sit here and see mountains that are miles away; the thought that we will soon be able to live within sight of these mountains fills us with optimism. We order a little wine and linger in the sunlight. Vancouver is going to be an adventure. We're going to be happy here. Marge Little, feeling expansive, tells us about her three children and about the problem she has keeping her weight down. "Marge Large they'll be calling me soon," she says. It's an old joke, we sense, and the telling of it makes us feel we're old friends. She got into the business, she says, because she loves houses. And she has an instinct for matching houses with people. "So don't be discouraged," she tells us. "We'll find the perfect place this afternoon."

We drive through narrow city streets to a house where a famous movie idol grew up. His mother still lives in the house, a spry, slightly senile lady in her eighties. The tiny house — we quickly see it is far too small for us — is crowded with photographs of the famous son. He beams at us from the hallway, from the dining room, from the bedroom bureau.

"Oh, he's a good boy. Comes home every two or three years," his mother tells us, her large teeth shining in a diminished face. "And once I went down there, all the way down to Hollywood, on an airplane. He paid my way, sent me a ticket. I saw his swimming pool. They all have swimming pools. He has a cook, a man who does all the meals, so I didn't have to lift a finger for a whole week. What an experience, like a queen. I have some pictures someplace I could show you —"

"That would be wonderful," Marge Little says, "but" — she glances at her watch — "I'm afraid we have another appointment."

"— I saw those pictures just the other day. Now where —? I think they're in this drawer somewhere. Here, I knew it. Take a look at this. Isn't that something? That's his swimming pool. Kidney-shaped. He's got another one now, even bigger."

"Beautiful," Ivy says.

"And here he is when he was little. See this? He'd be about nine there. We took a trip east. That's him and his dad standing by Niagara Falls. Here's another —"

"We really have to —"

"A good boy. I'll say that for him. Didn't give any trouble. Sometimes I see his movies on the TV and I can't believe the things he does, with women and so on. I have to pinch myself and say it's only pretend —"

"I think —"

"I'm going into this senior-citizen place. They've got a nice TV lounge, big screen, bigger than this little bitty one, color too. I always —"

"Sad," Ivy says, when we escape at last and get into the car.

"The house or the mother?" I ask her.

"Both."

"At least it's not a D.H." (This has become our shorthand expression for divorce house.)

"Wait'll you see the next place," Marge Little says, swinging into traffic. "The next place is fabulous."

Fabulous, yes. But far too big. After that, in a fit of

desperation, we look at a condo. "I'm not quite ready for this," I have to admit.

"No garden," Ivy says in a numb voice. She looks weary, and we decide to call it a day.

The ad in the newspaper reads: *Well Loved Family Home.* And Ivy and Marge Little and I are there, knocking on the door at 9:30 a.m.

"Come in, come in," calls a young woman in faded jeans. She has a young child on one hip and another — they must be twins — by the hand. Sunlight pours in the front window and there is freshly baked bread cooling on the kitchen counter.

But the house is a disaster, a rabbit warren of narrow hallways and dark corners. The kitchen window is only feet away from a low brick building where bodywork is being done on imported sportscars. The stairs are uneven. The bedroom floors slope and the paint is peeling off the bathroom ceiling.

"It just kills us to leave this place," the young woman says. She's following us through the rooms, pointing with unmistakable sorrow at the wall where they were planning to put up shelving, at the hardwood floors they were thinking of sanding. Out of the blue, they got news of a transfer.

Ironically, they're going to Toronto, and in a week's time they'll be there doing what we're doing, looking for a house they can love. "But we just know we'll never find a place like this," she tells us with sad shake of her head. "Not in a million zillion years."

After that we lose track of the number of houses. The day bends and blurs; square footage, zoning regulations, mortgage schedules, double-car garages, cedar-siding only two years old — was that the place near that little park? No, that was the one on that little crescent off Arbutus. Remember? The one without the basement.

Darkness is falling as Marge Little drives us back to our hotel. We are passing hundreds — it seems like thousands — of houses, and we see lamps being turned on, curtains being closed. Friendly smoke rises from substantial chimneys. Here and there, where the curtains are left open, we can see people sitting down to dinner. Passing one house I see a woman in a window, leaning over with a match in her hand, lighting a pair of candles. Ivy sees it too, and I'm sure she's feeling as I am, a little resentful that everyone but us seems to have a roof overhead.

"Tomorrow for sure," Marge calls cheerily. (Tomorrow is our last day. Both of us have to be home on Monday.)

"I suppose we could always rent for a year." Ivy says this with low enthusiasm.

"Or," I say, "we could make another trip in a month or so. Maybe there'll be more on the market."

"Isn't it funny? The first house we saw, remember? In a way, it was the most promising place we've seen."

"The one with the view from the dining room? With the broken light in the bathroom?"

"It might not look bad with a new fixture. Or even a skylight."

"Wasn't that a divorce house?" I ask Ivy.

"Yes," she shrugs, "but maybe that's just what we'll just have to settle for."

"It *was* listed at a good price."

"I live in a divorce house," Marge Little says, pulling up in front of our hotel. "It's been a divorce house for a whole year now."

"Oh, Marge," Ivy says. "I didn't mean — "she stops. "Forgive me."

"And it's not so bad. Sometimes it's darned cheerful."

"I just — " Ivy takes a breath, "I just wanted a lucky house. Maybe there's no such thing — "

"Are you interested in taking another look at the first house? I might be able to get you an appointment this evening. That is, if you think you can stand one more appointment today."

"Absolutely," we say together.

This time we inspect the house inch by inch. Ivy makes a list of the necessary repairs and I measure the windows for curtains. We hadn't realized that there was a cedar closet off one of the bedrooms. The lights of the city are glowing through the dining-room window. A spotlight at the back of the house picks out the flowers just coming into bloom. There'll be room for our hi-fi across from the fireplace. The basement is dry and very clean. The wallpaper in the downstairs den is fairly attractive and in good condition. The stairway is well-proportioned and the banister is a beauty. (I'm a sucker for banisters.) There's an alcove where the pine buffet will fit nicely. Trees on both sides of the house should give us greenery and privacy. The lawn, as far as we can tell, seems to be in good shape. There's a lazy susan in the kitchen, also a built-in dishwasher, a later model than ours. Plenty of room for a small table and a couple of chairs. The woodwork in the living room has been left natural, a wonder since so many people, a few years back, were painting over their oak trim.

Ivy says something that makes us laugh. "Over here," she says, "over here is where we'll put the Christmas tree." She touches the edge of one of the casement windows, brushes it with the side of her hand, and says, "It's hard to believe that people could live in such a beautiful house and be unhappy."

For a moment there's silence, and then Marge says, "We could put in an offer tonight. I don't think it's too late. What do you think?"

And now, suddenly, it's the next evening, and Ivy and I are flying back to Toronto. Here we are over the Rockies again, crossing them this time in darkness. Ivy sits with her head back, eyes closed, her shoulders so sharply her own; she's not quite asleep, but not quite awake either.

Our plane seems a fragile vessel, a piece of jewelry up here between the stars and the mountains. Flying through dark air like this makes me think that life itself is fragile. The miniature accidents of chromosomes can spread unstoppable circles of grief. A dozen words carelessly uttered can dismantle a marriage. A few gulps of oxygen are all that stand between us and death.

I wonder if Ivy is thinking, as I am, of the three months

ahead, of how tumultuous they'll be. There are many things to think of when you move. For one, we'll have to put our own house up for sale. The thought startles me, though I've no idea why.

I try to imagine prospective buyers arriving for appointments, stepping through our front door with polite murmurs and a sharp eye for imperfections.

They'll work their way through the downstairs, the kitchen (renewed only four years ago), the living room (yes, a real fireplace, a good draft), the dining room (small, but you can seat ten in a pinch). Then they'll make their way upstairs (carpet a little worn, but with lots of wear left). The main bedroom is a fair size (with good reading lamps built in, also bookshelves).

And then there's Christopher's bedroom.

Will the vibrations announce that here lived a child with little muscular control, almost no sight or hearing, and no real consciousness as that word is normally perceived? He had, though — and perhaps the vibrations will acknowledge the fact — his own kind of valor and perhaps his own way of seeing the world. At least Ivy and I always rewallpapered his room every three years or so out of a conviction that he took some pleasure in the sight of ducks swimming on a yellow sea. Later, it was sailboats; then tigers and monkeys dodging jungle growth; then a wild op-art checkerboard; and then, the final incarnation, a marvellous green cave of leafiness with amazing flowers and impossible birds sitting in branches.

I can't help wondering if these prospective buyers, these people looking for God only knows what, if they'll enter this room and feel something of his fragile presence alive in a fragile world.

Well, we shall see. We shall soon see.

The Metaphor Is Dead — Pass It On

"THE METAPHOR IS DEAD," bellowed the gargantuan professor, his walrus mustache dancing and his thundery eyebrows knitting together rapaciously. "Those accustomed to lunching at the high table of literature will now be able to nosh at the trough on a streamlined sub minus the pickle. Banished is that imperial albatross, that dragooned double agent, that muddy mirror lit by the false flashing signal *like* and by that even more presumptuous little sugar lump *as*. The gates are open, and the prisoner, freed of his shackles, has departed without so much as a goodbye wave to those who would take a simple pomegranate and insist it be the universe.

"Furthermore," trumpeted the cagey professor, warming to his thesis and drumming on the lectern, "the dogged metaphor, that scurfy escort vehicle of crystalline simplicity, has been royally indicted as the true enemy of meaning, a virus introduced into a healthy bloodstream and maintained by the lordly shrewdness of convention. Oh, it was born innocently enough with Homer and his wine-dark sea (a timid offering perhaps but one that dropped a velvet curtain between what *was* and what *almost* was). Then came Beowulf stirring the pot with his cunning kennings, and before you could count to sixteen, the insidious creature had wiggled through the window and taken over the house. Soon it became a private addiction, a pipe full of opium taken behind a screen — but the wavelet graduated to turbulent ocean, and the sinews of metaphor became, finally, the button and braces that held up the pants of poesy. The commonest object was yoked by adulterous communion with unlike object (bread and wine, as it were, touching the salty lips of unreason like a capricious child who insists on placing a token toe in every puddle).

"Initially a toy of the literati," the fiery professor cried, "the metaphor grew like a polyp on the clean chamber of poetry whose friendly narrative lines had previously lain as simply as knives and forks in a kitchen drawer and whose slender, unjointed nouns, colloquial as onions, became puffed up like affected dowagers, swaying, pelvis forward, into a Victorian parlor of cluttered predicates where they took to sitting about on the embroidered cushions of metonymy and resting their metered feet on quirky mean-spirited oxymorons.

"Once established they acquired an air of entitlement, the swag and flounce and glitter of the image boxed within another image, one bleating clause mounting another, sometimes marinated in irony, other times drenched in the teacup of whimsy. Grown fat with simile and the lace of self-indulgence, the embryo sentence sprouted useless tentacles and became an incomprehensible polyhedron, a glassine envelope enclosing multiple darting allusions that gave off the perfume of apples slowly rotting in a hermit's cryptic cellar. There followed signs of severe hypochondria as these verbal clotheshorses stood contemplating one another and noting the inspired imbroglio lodged beneath each painted fingernail. The bell had clearly sounded. It was time to retreat.

"And now," the professor essayed, stabbing the listening air, "like light glancing off a bowling ball, the peeled, scrubbed and eviscerated simplicity of language is reborn. Out onto the rubbish heap goes the fisherman's net of foxy allusions. A lifeboat has been assigned to every passenger — and just in time, too — and we are once again afloat on the simple raft of the declarative sentence (that lapsed Catholic of the accessible forms) and sent, shriven and humble, into orbit, unencumbered by the debris of dusty satellites, no longer pretending every object is *like* another; instead every object *is* (*is*, that frosty little pellet of assertion which sleeps in the folds of the newly minted, nip-waisted sentence, simple as a slug bolt and, like a single hand clapping, requiring neither nursemaid to lean upon nor the succor of moth-eaten mythology to prop it up). With watercolor purity, with soldierly persistence and workmanlike lack of pretence, the newly pruned utterance appears to roll onto the snowy page with not a single troubling cul-de-sac or detour into the inky besmudged midnight of imagery.

"But, alas," the ashen professor hollowly concluded, "these newly resurrected texts, for all their lean muscularity (the cleanly gnawed bones of *noun*, the powerful hamstrings of *verb*) carry still the faulty chromosome, the trace element, of metaphor — since language itself is but a metaphoric expression of human experience. It is the punishing silence around the word that must now be claimed for literature, the pure uncobbled stillness of the caesura whose unknowingness throws arrows of meaning (palpable as summer fruit approaching ripeness) at the hem of that stitched underskirt of affirmation/negation, and plants a stout flag once and forever in the unweeded, unchoreographed vacant lot of being.

"And now, gentlepeople, the chair will field questions."

A Wood

(with Anne Shields)

THE OTHER EVENING Ross and Stanley arrived at the rehearsal hall in time to see Elke go through her violin concert to be performed at the end of the month. It has taken all these years for recognition to come, though she began composing when she was sixteen. How serene she looked in the middle of the bare stage. But she was wearing that damned peasant skirt; Ross had begged her not to dress like that. It made her look like a twelve-tone type. It made her look less than serious.

"Isn't she magnificent!" Stanley said, breathless. "The coloring! The expression! Like little gold threads pouring out."

"She'll never be ready," Ross said. "She should have been working all summer."

"You're hard on her. Don't be hard on her. She's human. She needed to get away."

"We're all hard on each other, all the Woods are hard on each other. Papa used to say, 'A Wood will only settle for standards of excellence. A Wood asks more of himself than he asks of others.'"

Stanley hadn't thought of poor Papa for some months, and now he joined in. "A Wood knows that work is the least despised of human activities."

"Shhhh," Ross said. "She's starting her *Chanson des Fleurs*."

"A Wood values accomplishment above all," said Stanley who, now that he had started, couldn't stop.

"Shhhh."

The first searching notes of the song were spirited from the instrument. Elke heard each note as a reproach. She hadn't yet seen her two brothers in the back row; the lights at the top of the stage were on, blinding her. The song was coarse and coppery, not as it sounded when she wrote it. Why did she write it? How could she expect substance to come out of nothing?

The violin dug uncompromisingly into the soft flesh of her neck and chin. Today the bow seemed malicious and sharp. These benign forms — she had let them take her over and become something else. The song, mercifully, ended, and so did her dark thoughts.

"Bravo, Encore." Stanley's voice rang out. Was he here then? If only they'd shut off the lights. Why would they need them on so long before the actual concert? Today wasn't even a real rehearsal. How had Stanley tracked her down? If only it could be hoped that he hadn't brought Ross.

"Stanley?" Her wavery voice. It was a good thing she hadn't been trained as an actress. "Was that you, love?"

At the restaurant Elke was drinking red wine instead of white because Ross said it was more calming for her; she could scarcely afford to have one of her spells with the concert so near at hand. And only one glass, said Ross, then she must go home and get a good night's sleep.

Stanley watched her closely, thinking how regal she was. The long Wood nose. The Wood eyes. An almost Wood chin, but less resolute than his or Ross', which was perhaps a good thing.

"Well, of course I'm glad you came," she was saying to Stanley. "But who told you where the rehearsal hall was? Ross, I suppose."

"When you played the *Danse de Feu* I had tears in my eyes," Stanley said. "Even now, two hours later, just thinking about it brings back tears."

Ross said, "But you always cry at concerts."

"And at art galleries," said Elke. "I remember taking you to the Picasso retrospective at the Art Gallery when you were fifteen and you got weepy and had to go to the men's room.''

"Papa cried when he heard Callas," Ross said. "You could hear him sniffling all over the balcony.''

Elke turned to Stanley and touched the top of his wrist. "Promise me you won't cry at the concert. I don't know what I'd do if I heard someone blowing into a handkerchief from the third row. I'd lose my place. I'd lose my sense of balance.''

"I can't promise," Stanley said, his eyes filling with tears.

Elke found it hard to breathe. She was overwhelmed the way she had been with Papa before the accident. There was Ross, so brusque and demanding. And Stanley, too sweet, too sweet. The two were inseparable and, it seemed lately, inescapable. She would have to invent strategies to keep them out.

"Do you believe," she asked them, "do you believe that there is hidden meaning in what we dream?''

"Oh, yes," said Stanley at once.

Ross poured himself another glass of his chilled, ivory-colored wine.

"Well," Elke began, "I'll tell you my dream then, and you must interpret it for me." The only question in her mind was which dream to describe. She chose the one that they might be most likely to understand.

"Papa gave me, in this dream, a set of heavy, leather-bound books. They were encyclopedia, very old and very valuable. They filled the long shelf above my desk. One day, as I sat looking through volume R to S, I noticed that the binding, under the leather, was made of old sheet music. I was certain that this was one of Schiffmann's lost symphonies, although I don't know why I was so sure of this. So, of course, I ripped apart every book and peeled away the pages of the symphony. And just as I became aware that I was mistaken, that the music was only a series of piano exercises, I also became aware that you and Papa had come into the room and were looking at me with expressions of enormous reproach.''

•

"She made it up," Ross said later when he and Stanley had turned out the light and were about to go to sleep. "She made up the whole dream."

From the other side of the room Stanley's voice was muffled. He liked to pull the blanket up so that it reached his lips. "How do you know it wasn't a real dream?"

"Woods don't dream, at least not dreams as vivid or as detailed as that. Besides, I talked to her psychiatrist after the last episode, and he told me she made up dreams all the time."

"I have dreams," said Stanley.

"She makes up dreams in order to reinforce her image of herself as a victim. In her made-up dreams there is always someone shouting at her or scolding her or pointing out her faults. In one of the dreams Papa was telling her she'd ruined her career because she'd cut her hair. It took all the creative force out of her."

"Like Sampson," Stanley said.

"There was another dream, more extreme, when Papa was accusing her of causing his accident. She invited him to supper, and then she phoned and told him not to come after all; she was too tired even to make him an omelet. That was how he happened to be wandering down Sherbrooke on his way to the delicatessen when the motorbike knocked him down. Of course, it was all invented. She prefers to think she's the guilty cause of disaster. You might say she's greedy for guilt. But she didn't fool the psychiatrist at all. Real dreams have a different texture, and he's convinced Elke never really dreamed these dreams."

"I have dreams," Stanley said.

Elke started awake so suddenly her left leg cramped beneath her. Gently she kneaded at the hard knot in her calf. The window was open and the moon floated full and fat as though for her inspection. Last summer she'd been sent to study in Paris, and in the bank where she'd gone to change her grant checks there had been a sign: *DEMANDEZ-VOUS LA LUNE.* Of course she never did. Instead, she'd spent the tissuey franc notes and the long August afternoons in the café nearest her hotel.

She was seized, as always, in the middle of the night by regrets. She'd been so close to something original; it had flickered at the edge of her vision, in one of the darker corners of the café.

She must try to sleep. She would have to focus her energy and try to concentrate, if only for their sake. At least they found her worth their trouble. That was something.

"Too much, too much." She whispered these words out loud.

Then she slept, and her head again filled with dreams.

Despite being a Wood, Stanley had at least one vivid little dream every night. In the morning, as soon as he woke, he wrote a summary in a spiral-bound notebook. Sometimes he dreamed of food, chiefly artichokes, which he loved immoderately; sometimes he dreamed of music; and very frequently he dreamed of wandering down corridors with labyrinthine rooms going off to the left and right. He never dreamed about Papa. In fact, he seldom thought about him for weeks at a time, and he was naturally a little ashamed of this.

But he excused himself; he was busy. He woke early every day, drank a glass of hot tea and was in his workroom by eight-thirty. He had a great many orders — everyone seemed suddenly to want a handmade guitar. A student from a technical school helped him in the afternoons. They talked as they worked, which Stanley found charming. At 4:45, he locked the door and walked the mile and a half to the concert hall in order to catch the end of Elke's rehearsal. Usually, Ross was there when he arrived, sitting with a copy of the score on his lap and holding a little penlight so he could see in the dark.

One day after the rehearsal, a week before the performance, Stanley slipped Elke a note. "Dear Elke," it read. "The night before Papa's accident I forgot to remind him to take his heart pill. You remember how forgetful he was. I am certain that he had a heart attack on the way to the delicatessen and collapsed just as the motorbike came around the corner. Love, Stanley."

Elke was too tired to read yet another of Stanley's little notes. She accepted it with a small smile, then slipped it between the sheets of music on her stand. She never saw it again and assumed that it had fallen during the night and been swept up and thrown away — which was what she would have done with it herself.

In any case, the note wouldn't have comforted her. She worried less about the actual cause of Papa's death than everyone thought. It was what he'd meant to her that she fretted about, and his expectations. Her psychiatrist had assured her that the death would release her, but she knew she was going through with the concert for Papa's sake. For Papa, everything must be flawless.

Stanley told her her playing was perfect. It was impossible for her to improve. "Don't change a thing," he begged.

Ross told her he would select her clothes for the concert. He had examined her wardrobe. Only the red blouse would, perhaps, do. She needed a skirt, shoes, a scarf — everything. She was not to worry about it. He would look for the clothes and would buy her what she needed.

Elke found herself thanking him.

Ross was happy. Stanley had not seen him so happy since before Papa died. He smiled; he pranced; he showed Stanley the new clothes which he'd spread out on his bed. (Once this had been Papa's bed.)

There was a long black skirt made of some silky material, a pair of black shoes which consisted of thin little straps, and a printed scarf with red fleurs-de-lis on a black background.

That night, however, Stanley dreamed that the scarf became wound around Elke's neck during the performance and strangled her. He said to Ross in the morning, "I like everything but the scarf. Elke should wear the gold necklace instead of a scarf."

"It's too heavy for Elke," Ross said.

"It might bring her luck," said Stanley.

Many generations of Woods had worn the gold necklace. Three Woods had been married in it. A Wood had worn it to a funeral mass for Czar Nicholas. A Wood had shaken the hand of the great Schiffmann while wearing it. A Wood had hidden it behind a plaster wall in the city of Berlin. Another Wood had carried it out of Spain in 1936 sewn into the hem of a blanket.

"Gold can be vulgar," said Ross. "A scarf has more *esprit*."

"Papa would have insisted she wear the necklace," said Stanley. He was tired. He'd worked later than usual.

"All right," Ross said. "Tomorrow I'll go to the bank and get it out of the vault. But don't tell Elke. I want to surprise her."

On the day of the concert, Elke woke refreshed and alert after what seemed to her to have been a dream-free night. She lay for a few minutes in her bed and tried to remember when she'd last felt so almost happy. Her bedroom was filled with sunny shades of yellow and red — colors she'd chosen herself. The room was quiet. She could lie here as long as she wanted, and no one would come to tell her to get up.

She was at the hall by noon, before the technicians, before her brothers, before the audience and critics. Today the stage felt friendly; it welcomed the sound of her steps and her soft humming of the music she would play tonight. There was no terror in this.

"How do you feel?" Ross's voice sounded sharply at her feet. He was standing, suddenly, at the stairs leading from the front row to the stage. "Did you sleep well?"

"Woods always sleep well." Her rare teasing voice.

"But *did* you?" He paused, then walked up the stairs to where she was standing. His arms stretched toward her in a curious, beseeching gesture. "I've brought you the necklace. I got it from the bank yesterday, just before it closed for the weekend. I was so worried, I hid it underneath my pillow all night."

"Are you sure — ?" Elke asked.

"Papa would have wanted you to wear it."

"Then I must, of course."

"Hurry," Ross said to Stanley. "We want to be there at least twenty minutes before the program begins."

"I should polish my shoes one more time," said Stanley. The two brothers stood by the door, dressed alike in their black suits and dark ties, the coarse Wood hair brushed back from their foreheads.

"Your shoes are fine as they are," Ross said, but he did not want to start a quarrel. He had quarreled with Papa the night he died, a circuitous quarrel about bonds and about the little Monet drawing — what should be done with it. It was just after the quarrel, in fact, that Papa had rushed out into the street and fallen in the path of the motorcyclist.

"I'll only be a minute," Stanley said. He found a soft cloth and rubbed at the toes of his black shoes. Then he pulled at his shirt cuffs and examined them. Elke must be proud of them tonight.

The air outside was spicy and cold, and the chilly white light of the moon coated the pavement and the tops of parked cars. Ross and Stanley fell into step, left-right, left-right. They were silent, guarding their thoughts and guarding at the same time, it seemed, Elke's good luck. Stanley wondered if she were anxious, if the little nerves were jumping under the skin of her playing arm, if she were finding it painful to breathe, if her vision were blurred or her thoughts scattered.

Walking along dark streets always made Stanley think of how piteously men and women struggle to make themselves known to one another, how lonely they can be.

At least he wasn't alone. He would never be alone. Thinking this, he stumbled slightly with happiness and bumped up against Ross. The two of them bounced lightly off each other as two eggs will do when boiled in a little pan.

Elke had persuaded Ross and Stanley to let her eat supper alone. She ate two peeled peaches and a bowl of cornflakes, and had drunk a small glass of Scotch. Now she was wandering the corridors beneath the stage.

There seemed an endless number of rooms: dressing rooms

like her own, larger rooms filled with props and costumes, one tiny room with row after row of wigs, several rooms of mops and rags and buckets, then a little library whose shelves were weighted down with scripts and scores, next a delightful room full of instruments in need of repair, and still another room full of instruments beyond repair. This labyrinth of rooms had the surprising and inevitable logic of a dream.

She glanced at the watch given to her by Papa for her last birthday; the slim gold pointers had moved alarmingly fast. She had only a few minutes to get dressed. Before turning back to her room where Ross's clothes lay spread out on a divan waiting for her, Elke opened one last door.

Costumes, costumes. These must be the costumes for the Saturday matinee performances of fairy tales given to busloads of children; Rapunzel's gown, Goldilocks' frilled pinafore, Sleeping Beauty's nightdress, Cinderella's slippers, Red Riding Hood's cape. The costumes were made to last for years of performances, and were lovely enough to enchant the most disenchanted of children. Rapunzel's gold-green gown, with its square neck and high empire waist, was by far the most beautiful and, as it happened, fit Elke perfectly.

The gold necklace, retrieved from a hiding place in her dressing room, sat solidly on her throat, framed by the square of satin and velvet. Elke caught up her violin and bow and walked lightly up to the wings.

"Four more minutes."

"Five. Shhhh."

"A worthy audience. A very fine audience. Wouldn't you say so, Ross? A fine audience?"

"Well, of course. A Wood always — "

"Ross?"

"What?"

"Papa."

"What about Papa?"

"Do you think he — ? Do you ever believe that...after people die, that they — "

"Yes."

"Yes, what? You mean you think — ?"

"Yes, I'm sure of it. Papa is here. With us. Tonight."

"I don't."

"What do you mean, you don't?"

"I don't think he's here."

"Of course he's here."

"I think he's gone. I'm sure of it. He's left us."

"He'll never leave us."

"Isn't that — ?"

"Yes. Shhhh. She's coming."

Elke had just arrived in the wings when the lights were dimmed and the noise from the audience thinned to a softer sound. She stood, bent slightly forward, with one arm crooked around the violin and the bow held lightly in the opposite hand. Under the surprising folds of the costume, which she now realized smelled strongly of mothballs and dust, her body felt cool and determined.

It seemed suddenly as though Papa were near — in the chamber of the violin or wrapped around the resined strings of her bow. But she knew this was only an illusion stirred by the hard lights and the rising excitement.

"He's gone," she told herself, looking down at the backs of her hands. "I'm sure of that, at least."

It was time to begin. It was past time to begin. A hand pressed on her spine between her neck and her waist, between her shoulder blades, an encouraging, insistent pressure. "Go, go, they are waiting."

Elke bent her neck to show she was ready, then followed the angle of her head out onto the stage. A few minutes of surging noise — was someone shouting something to her? — then she laid her chin and her cheek on the violin, positioned her arm and bow. She closed her eyes and clearly saw the notes of her *Chanson des Fleurs* lined up before her. With a slight nod to the notes, to the audience, to herself, to whomever might be watching, she began to play.

Stanley was on his feet. "Bravo! Bravissimo!"

The two, bright, flag-shaped words were out of his mouth before he realized it and before Elke had played a single note. The shame, the shame. He felt the blood go out of his clapping hands and then their unbearable weight at his sides. The disgrace! For Elke, for Ross, for Papa whose wide pale disappointed face came sliding before his eyes.

To himself he said: "I'm going to faint."

But he didn't. All around him people were rising to their feet and applauding. For Elke, darling Elke. Even Ross, looking stunned, rose and opened his mouth and whispered, "Bravo."

She began. Her *Chanson* first, each note rounded like the bowl of a spoon. Stanley held his breath in the final bars where the notes seemed to heap themselves one on top of the other. Then, her *August Suite* and, after that, her *Fleuve Noir*, so slow, so stately that Stanley would have cried if he hadn't felt carried to a calm rivery place beyond tears. Last, Elke played her silky little *Lament* in memory of Papa.

She bowed deeply. It was the intermission already. The gold necklace burned at her throat and the great golden-green dress swept the floor — where had she found such a dress? Stanley turned to ask Ross, who was staring straight ahead, "Where has she found such a dress?"

"We picked it out together," Ross was saying. "It seemed to set off the necklace."

It was over. She was back in the dressing room, exhausted, happy, her fingers aching for the resistance of the strings, her heart rocking. All those people; all those eyes scraping against the skin of her face.

She hesitated only a moment before opening the door to Ross's knock. One, two, three, she counted, then opened it.

Stanley followed Ross into the room carrying — by the stems, heads downward — an enormous bouquet of flowers, an absurd bouquet of flowers. "Ecstasies! Ecstasies!" His eyes rolled, his arms swung, and the flowers fell to the floor, their sharp fragrance mingling with the odor of mothballs.

Ross blinked, then smiled, then bent down and picked up the

strewn flowers. "For you," he said, presenting them and kissing Elke in the Wood way, first on one check, then on the other, finally on the forehead. "You are a true Wood," he said into her ear. He did not look into her eyes.

"The truest Wood," added Stanley, who liked the last word, and who was always permitted to have it.

Love so Fleeting,
Love so Fine

WENDY IS BACK! the sign said. It caught his eye.

It was a handprinted sign and fairly crude — not that he was a man who objected to crudeness; crayon lettering on a piece of cardboard: WENDY IS BACK! it said.

The sign was in the window of an orthopedic shoe store on a dim back street in downtown Winnipeg. He passed it one morning on his way to the office, and the image of the sign, and all the questions it raised, stayed with him, printed as it were on the back wall of his eye.

Who is Wendy?

Where has she been?

Why is she back?

And why is her return the cause of joy?

Joy, there was no other word for it. The sign taped flat against the plate-glass window was a joyful announcement, a public proclamation, reinforced, too, by its light, high floater of an exclamation point (that fond crayoned slash of exuberance) testifying to the fact that Wendy's return, whether from visiting her grandmother in Portage or from vacationing with a girlfriend in Hawaii, was an event worthy of celebration. The question was, why?

She would be about his own age, he reasoned — which was thirty. Nobody over thirty was named Wendy, at least nobody he'd ever met. But where had she been? Perhaps she'd been sick; flu was going the rounds, a persistent strain. (He himself had missed three days at work only the week before, and now his wife had come down with it.) Or an operation. Impossible.

It was more likely that she'd been sent away to Toronto or Montreal or St. Catharines for a job-upgrading course at some obscure community college specializing in the modern fitting of difficult feet. He mused, as he walked along, on what a narrow speciality it must be, the fitting of orthopedic footwear, but necessary, of course, and how, like chimney cleaning and piano tuning, it was a vocation whose appeal to youth might not be immediately apparent. Undoubtedly, she, Wendy, had come back from the east with a new sense of buoyancy, brimming with the latest theories and "tips," which she now felt eager to pass on to her customers.

It was easy to see that her popularity with customers was established. The store manager — a fatherly type — might even refer to it as "phenomenal." (Else, why this sign in his window? And why the Christmas bonus already set aside for her?) Customers doubtless experienced an upsurge of optimism at the sight of her wide blue eyes or at hearing her cheery early morning "Hello there!" Her particular humor would be difficult to pin down, being neither dry nor wry nor witty, but consisting, rather, of a wink for the elderly gents and broad teasing compliments for the ladies — "These shoes'll put you right back in the chorus line, Mrs. Beamish." They loved it; they lapped it up; how could they help but adore Wendy.

"Our little Wendy's back," he imagined these old ones cackling one to another as they came in for fittings, "and about time too."

From North Winnipeg they came, from East Kildonan and Fort Garry and Southwood and even Brandon so that their warped and crooked and cosmically disfavored feet could be taken into Wendy's smooth young hands, examined minutely and murmered over — but in that merry little voice of hers that made people think of the daughters they'd never had. Into her care they could safely put the shame of their ancient bunions, their blue-black swollen ankles, their blistered heels. Her strong, unerring touch never shrank when it came to straightening out crippled toes or testing with her healthy thumbs that peculiar soft givingness that indicates a fallen arch. By sheer banter, by a kind of chiding playfulness, she absolved her clients of the rasp of old calluses, the yellowness of soles, the damp dishonor attached to foot odor, foot foulness, foot obloquy, foot ignominy.

All this and more Wendy was able to neutralize — with forehead prettily creased — by means of her steady, unflinching manner. These feet are only human, she would be ready to say if asked. Tarsus and metatarsus; corn, callus and nail; her touch is tender and without judgement. Willingly she rises from her little padded stool and fetches the catalogue sent from the supply house in Pittsburgh, and happily she points to Figure 42. "This little laced oxford doesn't look like much *off*," she concedes to Mrs. Beamish or whomever happens to be in her charge, "but it's really a very smart little shoe *on*."

He imagines that her working uniform is some kind of smock in a pastel shade, the nature of her work being, after all, primarily medical. A caring profession. A caring person. A person one cared about. Wendy! She was back!

And he loved her.

He admitted it to himself. Oh yes, it was like light spilling through a doorway, his love for her. Arriving at work and traveling in the elevator to the eleventh floor, he kept his eyes lowered, searching the feet of his fellow workers, noting here and there sturdy, polished, snub-nosed models with thickish heels. Had these people felt his Wendy's warm ministrations? He might, if he were bolder, announce loudly, "Wendy is back!" as if it were an oblation, and watch as smiles of recognition, then euphoria and a kind of relief, too, spread across their faces.

Later, alone, at the end of the work day, while his wife lay reading the newspaper in bed, he examined his own feet under a strong light. Would they soon require professional attention? Might they benefit from extra bracing or support, a foam lift at the heel, say, or — well, whatever Wendy would care to suggest now that she was up on the latest theories from the east. But what could he say to her that would not seem callow or self-serving or, worse, a plea for her attention. She might look at his two feet, stripped of their socks and laid bare and damp, and suspect he had come because of ulterior motives. Namely love. He is sure she is vigilant against those who would merely love her.

He is a man who has been in love many times. Before the transfer to the Winnipeg office, he spent two years in Vancouver, and once, standing in line at a bakery on 41st Avenue, he found himself behind two solemn young women who were ordering a farewell cake for a friend. "What would you like written on top?" the woman behind the counter asked them. They paused, looked uncertain, regarded each other, and then one of them said decisively, "So long, Louise."

Louise. Gold hair set off by a blue cotton square. Louise was leaving. Instinctively, he felt she didn't really want to go. All her friends were here. This was a beautiful city. She had a decent job, a pleasant apartment full of thick-leaved plants and bamboo furniture; she had a modest view of the mountains and a membership in a health club, but nevertheless she was leaving. SO LONG, LOUISE the pink icing on her farewell cake spelled out.

Something had forced the move on her — a problem that might be professional or personal, and now she would have to deal — alone, for how could he help her? — with storing her furniture, canceling her subscriptions, and giving away to friends the books and oddments she loved. Her medical insurance would have to be transferred, and there would be the last heartbreaking task of going down to the post office to arrange to have her mail forwarded. It seemed unpardonable to ask so much of a young woman who barely had had time to savor her independence and to study love's ingenious rarefaction. She would have to face the horror of apartment-hunting elsewhere; a whole new life to establish, in fact. If only he could put his arms around her, his poor Louise, whom he suddenly realized he cared deeply, deeply, deeply about.

His lost Louise. That is how he thinks of her, a woman standing in the airport — no, the bus station — in her dark cloth coat of good quality and her two pieces of soft-sided luggage in which lay folded a number of pale wool skirts and sweaters, and her little zippered bag of cosmetics, toiletries, talcum powder and emery boards which would be traveling, ineluctably, with her out to the edges of the city and over the mountain ranges and away from his yet-to-be declared love.

Still, he won't forget her, just as he has never forgotten his young and lovely Sherri, whom he first encountered thirty miles north of Kingston — where his first transfer took him. There he had seen, spray-painted in red on a broad exposed rock face, the message HANK LOVES SHERRI. It had been the coldest of March days; the countryside was an unrelenting gray, and he, driving along the highway, found himself longing for a sign of life, anything at all. A moment later he had swung around a curve and confronted HANK LOVES SHERRI in letters that were at least three feet high.

He knows, of course, what the Hanks of the world are like: loud-mouthed and jealous, with the beginnings of a beer belly, the kind of lout who believes the act of love was invented to cancel out the attachment of the spirit, the sort of person who might dare to fling a muscled, possessive arm across Sherri's shoulders while coming out of a coffee shop on Princess Street and later swear at her that she was different from the other girls he'd known. *His* Sherri, who, with her hyacinth cologne and bitten nails, was easily, fatally, impressed by male joviality and dark sprinklings of chest hairs. She would never stand a chance. For a while, a few months, she might be persuaded that Hank really did love her in his way, and that she, in return, loved him. But familiarity, intimacy — those enemies of love — would intervene, and one day she would wake up and find that something inside her had withered, that core of sweet vulnerability that was what *he* had loved in her from the first day when HANK LOVES SHERRI had stopped him cold on the highway.

And now it's Wendy who sets off wavelets of heat in his chest. WENDY IS BACK! He walks by the orthopedic footwear store again the next day — but this time more slowly. The loose leather wrappings on his feet scrape the pavement absurdly. His breath comes with pleasure and difficulty as though the air has been unbearably sweetened by her name — Wendy, Wendy, Wendy. Of course, he is tempted to peer closely through the dark plate glass, but finds it to be full of reflections — his own mainly, his hungry face. He might go in — not today, but tomorrow — on the pretext of asking the time or begging change for the parking meter or telephone. He'll think of something. Love invents potent strategies, and people in love are resourceful as well as devious. Wendy, Wendy is back. But for how long?

The end of his love affairs always brings a mixed nightmare of poignancy and the skirmishings of pain. He feels stranded, beached, with salt in his ears. What is over, is over; he is realist enough to recognize that. But his loves, Sherri, Louise, Wendy — and the others — never desert him entirely. He has committed to memory the minor physics of veneration and, on dark nights, after his wife has fallen asleep and lies snoring quietly beside him, he likes to hang on to consciousness for an extra minute or two and listen to the sound of the wind rocking the treetops and brushing silkily against the window. It's then he finds himself attended by a false flicker on the retina — some would say vision — in which long, brightly colored ribbons dance and sway before him. Their suppleness, their undulations, cut deeply into his heart and widen for an instant the eye of the comprehended world. Often he can hear, as well, the muted sound of female voices and someone calling out to him by name.

Dolls, Dolls, Dolls, Dolls

DOLLS. Roberta has written me a long letter about dolls, or more specifically about a doll factory she visited when she and Tom were in Japan.

"Ha," my husband says, reading her letter and pulling a face, "another pilgrimage to the heart's interior." He can hardly bring himself to read Roberta's letters anymore, though they come addressed to the two of us; there is a breathlessness about them that makes him squirm, a seeking, suffering openness which I suspect he finds grotesque in a woman of Roberta's age. Forty-eight, an uneasy age. And Roberta has never been what the world calls an easy woman. She is one of my oldest friends, and the heart of her problem, as I see it, is that she is incredulous, still, that the color and imagination of our childhood should have come to rest in nothing at all but these lengthy monochrome business trips with her husband, a man called Tom O'Brien; but that is neither here nor there.

In this letter from Japan, she describes a curious mystical experience that caused her not exactly panic and not precisely pleasure, but that connected her for an instant with an area of original sensation, a rare enough event at our age. She also unwittingly stepped into one of my previously undeclared beliefs. Which is that dolls, dolls of all kinds — those strung-together parcels of wood or plastic or cloth or whatever — possess a measure of energy beyond their simple substance, something half-willed and half-alive.

Roberta writes that Tokyo was packed with tourists; the weather was hot and humid, and she decided to join a touring party on a day's outing in the countryside — Tom was tied up in meetings, as per usual.

They were taken by air-conditioned bus to a village where ninety percent — the guide vigorously repeated this statistic — where ninety percent of all the dolls in Japan were made. "It's a major industry here," Roberta writes, and some of the dolls still were manufactured almost entirely by hand in a kind of cottage-industry system. One house in the village, for example, made nothing but arms and legs, another the bodies; another dressed the naked doll bodies in stiff kimonos of real silk and attached such objects as fans and birds to the tiny laquered female fingers.

Roberta's party was brought to a small house in the middle of the village where the heads of geisha dolls were made. Just the heads and nothing else. After leaving their shoes in a small darkened foyer, they were led into a surprisingly wide, matted workroom which was cooled by slow-moving overhead fans. The air was musty from the mingled straw and dust, but the light from a row of latticed windows was softly opalescent, a distinctly mild, non-industry quality of light, clean-focused and just touched with the egg-yellow of sunlight.

Here in the workroom nine or ten Japanese women knelt in a circle on the floor. They nodded quickly and repeatedly in the direction of the tourists, and smiled in a half-shy, half-neighborly manner; they never stopped working for a second.

The head-making operation was explained by the guide, who was a short and peppy Japanese with soft cheeks and a sharp "arfing" way of speaking English. First, he informed them, the very finest sawdust of a rare Japanese tree was taken and mixed with an equal solution of the purest rice paste. (Roberta writes that he rose up on his toes when he reached the words *finest* and *purest* as though paying tribute to the god of superlatives.) This dough-like material then was pressed into wooden molds of great antiquity (another toe-rising here) and allowed to dry very slowly over a period of days. Then it was removed and painted; ten separate and exquisitely thin coats of enamel were applied, so that the resulting form, with only an elegant nose breaking the white egg surface, arrived at the weight and feel and coolness of porcelain.

The tourists — hulking, Western, flat-footed in their bare feet — watched as the tiny white doll heads were passed around the circle of workers. The first woman, working with tweezers and glue, applied the eyes, pressing them into place with a small wooden stick. A second woman painted in the fine red shape of a mouth, and handed on the head to a woman who applied to the center of the mouth a set of chaste and tiny teeth. Other women touched the eyes with shadow, the cheeks with bloom, the bones with highlight, so that the flattened oval took on the relief and contours of sculptured form. "Lovely," Roberta writes in her letter, "a miracle of delicacy."

And finally, the hair. Before the war, the guide told them, real hair had been used, human hair. Nowadays a very fine quality of blue-black nylon was employed. The doll's skull was cunningly separated into two sections so that the hair could be firmly, permanently rooted from the inside. Then the head was sealed again, and the hair arranging began. The two women who performed this final step used real combs and brushes, pulling the hair smoothly over their hands so that every strand was in alignment, and then they shaped it, tenderly, deftly, with quick little strokes, into the intricate knots and coils of traditional geisha hair dressing.

Finally, at the end of this circular production line, the guide held up a finished head and briefly propagandized in his sharp, gingery, lordly little voice about the amount of time that went into making a head, the degree of skill, the years of apprenticeship. Notice the perfection of the finished product, he instructed. Observe the delicacy, mark the detailing. And then, because Roberta was standing closest to him, he placed the head in her hands for a final inspection.

And that was the moment Roberta was really writing me about. The finished head in her hands, with its staring eyes and its painted veil of composure and its feminine, almost erotic crown of hair, had more than the weight of artifact about it. Instinctively Roberta's hands had cupped the head into a laced cradle, protective and cherishing. There was something *alive* about the head.

An instant later she knew she had overreacted. "Tom always says I make too much of nothing," she apologizes. The head hadn't moved in her hands; there had been no sensation of pulse or breath, no shimmer of aura, no electrical charge, nothing. Her eyes went to the women who had created this little head. They smiled, bowed, whispered, miming a busy humility, but their cool waiting eyes informed her that they knew exactly what she was feeling.

What she *had* felt was a stirring apprehension of possibility. It was more than mere animism; the life, or whatever it was that had been brought into being by those industriously toiling women, seemed to Roberta to be deliberate and to fulfill some unstated law of necessity.

She ends her letter more or less the way she ends all her letters these days: with a statement that is really a question. "I don't suppose," she says, "that you'll understand any of this."

Dolls, dolls, dolls, dolls. Once — I forget why — I wrote those words on a piece of paper, and instantly they swam into incomprehension, becoming meaningless ruffles of ink, squiggles from a comic strip. Was it a Christmas wish list I was making? I doubt it. As a child I would have been shocked had I received more than one doll in a single year; the idea was unworthy, it was *unnatural*. I could not even imagine it.

Every year from the time I was born until the year I was ten I was given a doll. It was one of the certainties of life, a portion of a large, enclosing certainty in which all the jumble of childhood lay. It now seems a long way back to those particular inalterable surfaces: the vast and incomprehensible war; Miss Newbury, with her ivory-colored teeth, who was principal of Lord Durham Public School; Euclid Avenue where we lived in a brown house with a glassed-in front porch; the seasons with their splendors and terrors curving endlessly around the middle eye of the world which I shared with my sister and my mother and father.

Almost Christmas: there they would be, my mother and father at the kitchen table on a Saturday morning in early December, drinking drip coffee and making lists. There would come a succession of dark, chilly pre-Christmas afternoons in which the air would grow rich with frost and longing, and on one of those afternoons our mother would take the bus downtown to buy the Christmas dolls for my sister and me.

She loved buying the Christmas dolls, the annual rite of choosing. It's the faces, she used to say, that matter, those dear molded faces. She would be swept away by a pitch of sweetness in the pouting lips, liveliness and color in the lashed eyes, or a line of tenderness in the tinted cheeks — "The minute I laid eyes on that face," she would say, helplessly shaking her head in a way she had, "I just went and fell head over heels."

We never, of course, went with her on these shopping trips, but I can see how it must have been: Mother, in her claret-wine coat with the black squirrel collar, bending over, peering into glass cases in the red-carpeted toy department and searching in the hundreds of stiff smiling faces for a flicker of response, an indication of some kind that this doll, this particular doll, was destined for us. Then the pondering over price and value — she always spent more than she intended — having just one last look around, and finally, yes, she would make up her mind.

She also must have bought on these late afternoon shopping excursions Monopoly sets and dominoes and sewing cards, but these things would have been carried home in a different spirit, for it seems inconceivable for the dolls, our Christmas dolls, to be boxed and jammed into shopping bags with ordinary toys; they must have been carefully wrapped — she would have insisted on double layers of tissue paper — and she would have held them in her arms, crackling in their wrappings, all the way home, persuaded already, as we would later be persuaded, in the reality of their small beating hearts. What kind of mother was this with her easy belief, her adherence to seasonal ritual? (She also canned peaches the last week in August, fifty quarts, each peach half turned with a fork so that the curve, round as a baby's cheek, gleamed lustrous through the blue grass. Why did she do that — go to all that trouble? I have no idea, not even the seed of an idea.)

The people in our neighborhood on Euclid Avenue, the real and continuing people, the Browns, the McArthurs, the Sheas, the Callahans, lived as we did, in houses, but at the end of our block was a large yellow brick building, always referred to by us as The Apartments. The Apartments, frilled at the back with iron fire escapes, and the front of the building solid with its waxed brown foyer, its brass mailboxes and nameplates, its important but temporary air. (These people only rent, our father had told us.) The children who lived in The Apartments were always a little alien; it was hard for us to believe in the real existence of children who lacked backyards of their own, children who had no fruit cellars filled with pickles and peaches. Furthermore, these families always seemed to be moving on after a year or so, so that we never got to know them well. But on at least one occasion I remember we were invited there to a birthday party given by a little round-faced girl, an only child named Nanette.

It was a party flowing with new pleasures. Frilled nutcups at each place. A square bakery cake with shells chasing each other around the edges. But the prizes for the games we played — Pin the Tail on the Donkey, Musical Chairs — were manipulated so that every child received one — was that fair? — and these prizes were too expensive, overwhelming completely the boxed handkerchiefs and hair ribbons we'd brought along as gifts. But most shocking of all was the present that Nanette received from her beaming parents.

We sat in the apartment under the light of a bridge lamp, a circle of little girls on the living-room rug, watching while the enormous box was untied. Inside was a doll.

What kind of doll it was I don't recall except that her bronzed hair gleamed with a richness that was more than visual; what I do remember was the affection with which she was lifted from her wrappings of paper and pressed to Nanette's smocked bodice, how she was tipped reverently backward so that her eyes clicked shut, how she was rocked to and fro, murmured over, greeted, kissed, christened. It was as though Nanette had no idea of the inappropriateness of this gift. A doll could only begin her life at Christmas. Was it the rigidities of my family that dictated this belief, or some obscure and unconscious approximation to the facts of gestation? A birthday doll, it seemed to me then, constituted a violation of the order of things, and it went without saying that the worth of all dolls was diminished as a result.

Still, there sat Nanette, rocking back and forth in her spun rayon dress, stroking the doll's stiff wartime curls and never dreaming that she had been swindled. Poor Nanette, there could be no heartbeat in that doll's misplaced body; it was not possible. I felt a twist of pity, probably my first, a novel emotion, a bony hand yanking at my heart, an emotion oddly akin — I see it clearly enough now — to envy.

In the suburbs of Paris is one of the finest archeological museums in Europe — my husband had talked, ever since I'd known him, about going there. The French, a frugal people, like to make use of their ancient structures, and this particular museum is housed inside a thirteenth-century castle. The castle, if you block out the hundreds of surrounding villas and acacia-lined streets, looks much as it always must have looked, a bulky structure of golden stone with blank, primitive, upswept walls and three round brutish towers whose massiveness might be a metaphor for that rough age which equated masonry with power.

The interior of this crude stone shell has been transformed by the Ministry of Culture into a purring, beige-toned shrine to modernism, hived with climate controlled rooms and corridors, costly showcases and thousands of artifacts, subtly lit, lovingly identified. The *pièce de résistance* is the ancient banqueting hall where today can be seen a wax reconstruction of pre-Frankish family life. Here in this room a number of small, dark, hairy manikins squat naked around a cleverly simulated fire. The juxtaposition of time — ancient, medieval and modern — affected us powerfully; my husband and young daughter and I stared for some time at this strange tableau, trying to reconcile these ragged eaters of roots with the sleek, meaty, well-clothed Parisians we'd seen earlier that day shopping on the rue Victor Hugo.

We spent most of an afternoon in the museum looking at elegantly mounted pottery fragments and tiny vessels, clumsily formed from cloudy glass. There was something restorative about seeing French art at this untutored level, something innocent and humanizing in the simple requirement for domestic craft. The Louvre had exhausted us to the glitter of high style and finish, and at the castle we felt as though the French had allowed a glimpse of their coarser, more likable selves.

"Look at that," my husband said, pointing to a case that held a number of tiny clay figures, thousands of years old. We looked. Some of them were missing arms, and a few were missing their heads, but the bodily form was unmistakable.

"They're icons," my husband said, translating the display card: "From the pre-Christian era."

"Icons?" our daughter asked, puzzled. She was seven that summer.

"Like little gods. People in those days worshipped gods made of clay or stone."

"How do you know?" she asked him.

"Because it says so," he told her. "*Icône.* That's the French word for icon. It's really the same as our word."

"Maybe they're dolls," she said.

"No. It says right here. Look. In those days people were all pagans and they worshipped idols. Little statues like these. They sort of held them in their hands or carried them with them when they went hunting or when they went to war."

"They could be dolls," she said slowly.

He began to explain again. "All the early cultures — "

She was looking at the figures, her open hand resting lightly on the glass case. "They look like dolls."

For a minute I thought he was going to go on protesting. His lips moved, took the necessary shape. He lifted his hand to point once again at the case. I felt sick with sudden inexplicable anger.

Then he turned to our daughter, shrugged, smiled, put his hands in his pocket. He looked young, twenty-five, or even younger. "Who knows," he said to her. "You might be right. Who knows."

My sister lives 300 miles away in Ohio, and these days I see her only two or three times a year, usually for family gatherings on long weekends. These visits tend to be noisy and clamorous. Between us we have two husbands and six children, and then there is the flurry of cooking and cleaning up after enormous holiday meals. There is never enough time to do what she and I love to do most, which is to sit at the kitchen table — hers or mine, they are interchangeable — with mugs of tea before us and to reconstruct, frame by frame, the scenes of our childhood.

My memory is sharper than hers, so that in these discussions, though I'm two years younger, I tend to lead while she follows. (Sometimes I long for a share of her forgetfulness, her leisured shrugging acceptance of past events. My own recollections, not all happy, are relentlessly present, kept stashed away like ingots, testifying to a peculiar imprisoning muscularity of recall.) The last time she came — early October — we talked about the dolls we had been given every Christmas. Our husbands and children listened, jealously it seemed to me, at the sidelines, the husbands bemused by this ordering of trivia, the children open-mouthed, disbelieving.

I asked my sister if she remembered how our dolls were presented to us, exactly the way real children are presented, the baby dolls asleep in stenciled cradles or wrapped in receiving blankets; and the schoolgirl dolls propped up by the Christmas tree, posed just so, smiling brilliantly and fingering the lower branches with their shapely curved hands. We always loved them on sight.

"Remember Nancy Lynn," my sister said. She was taking the lead this time. Nancy Lynn had been one of mine, one of the early dolls, a large cheerful baby doll with a body of cloth, and arms and legs of painted plaster. Her swirled brown hair was painted on, and at one point in her long life she took a hard knock on the head, carrying forever after a square chip of white at the scalp. To spare her shame we kept her lacy bonnet tied on day and night. (Our children, listening, howled at this delicacy.)

One wartime Christmas we were given our twin dolls, Shirley and Helen. The twins were small and hollow and made of genuine rubber, difficult to come by in those years of shortages, and they actually could be fed water from a little bottle. They were also capable of wetting themselves through tiny holes punched in their rubber buttocks; the vulnerability of this bodily process enormously enlarged our love for them. There was also Barbara the Magic Skin Doll, wonderfully pliable at first, though later her flesh peeled away in strips. There was a Raggedy Ann, not to our minds a real doll, but a cloth stuffed hybrid of good disposition. There was Brenda, named for her red hair, and Betty with jointed knees and a brave little tartan skirt. There was Susan — her full name was Brown-Eyed Susan — my last doll, only I didn't know it then.

My sister and I committed the usual sins, leaving our dolls in their pajamas for days on end, and then, with a rush of shame and love, scooping them up and trying to make amends by telescoping weeks and even years into a Saturday afternoon. Our fiercely loved dolls were left out in the rain. We always lost their shoes after the first month; their toes broke off almost invariably. We sometimes picked them up by the arm or even the hair, but we never disowned them or gave them away or changed their names, and we never buried them in ghoulish backyard funerals as the children in our English stories seemed to do. We never completely forgot that we loved them.

Our mother loved them too. What was it that stirred her frantic devotion? — some failure of ours? — some insufficiency in our household? She spent hours making elaborate wardrobes for them; both my sister and I can remember the time she made Brenda a velvet cape trimmed with scraps of fur from her old squirrel collar. Sometimes she helped us give them names: Patsy, Gloria, Merry Lu, Olivia.

"And the drawer," my sister said. "Remember the drawer?"

"What drawer?" I asked.

"You remember the drawer. In our dresser. That little drawer on the left-hand side, the second one down."

"What about it?" I asked slowly.

"Well, don't you remember? Sure you do. That's where our dolls used to sleep. Remember how Mother lined it with a doll blanket?"

"No," I said.

"She thumbtacked it all around, so it was completely lined. That's where Shirley and Helen used to sleep."

"Are you sure?"

"Absolutely."

I remind her of the little maple doll cribs we had.

"That was later," she said.

I find it hard to believe that I've forgotten about this, especially this. A drawer lined with a blanket; that was exactly the kind of thing I remembered.

But my sister still has the old dresser in the attic of her house. And she told me that the blanket still is tacked in place; she hasn't been able to bring herself to remove it. "When you come at Christmas," she said, "I'll show it to you."

"What color is it?" I asked.

"Pink. Pink with white flowers. Of course it's filthy now and falling apart."

I shook my head. A pink blanket with white flowers. I have no memory of such a blanket.

Perhaps at Christmas, when I actually look at the drawer, it all will come flooding back. The sight of it may unlock what I surely have stored away somewhere in my head, part of the collection of images which always has seemed so accessible and true. The fleecy pink drawer, the dark night, Shirley and Helen side by side, good night, good night as we shut them away. Don't let the bedbugs bite. Oh, oh.

It happened that in the city where I grew up a little girl was murdered. She was ten years old, my age.

It was a terrible murder. The killer had entered her bedroom window while she was sleeping. He had stabbed her through the heart; he cut off her head and her arms and her legs. Some of these pieces were never found.

It would have been impossible not to know about this murder; the name of the dead girl was known to everyone, and even today I have only to think the syllables of her name and the whole undertow of terror doubles back on me. This killer was a madman, a maniac who left notes in lipstick on city walls, begging the police to come and find him. He couldn't help himself. He was desperate. He threatened to strike again.

Roberta Callahan and JoAnn Brown and I, all of us ten years old, organized ourselves into a detective club and determined to catch the killer. We never played with dolls anymore. The Christmas before, for the first time, there had been no doll under the tree; instead, I had been given a wristwatch. My mother had sighed, first my sister, now me.

Dolls, which had once formed the center of my imagination, now seemed part of an exceedingly soft and sissified past, something I used to do before I got big. I had wedged Nancy Lynn and Brown-Eyed Susan and Brenda and Shirley and all the others onto a shelf at the back of my closet, and now my room was filled with pictures of horses and baseball stickers and collections of bird nests. Rough things, rugged things, tough things. For Roberta Callahan and JoAnn Brown and I desired, above all else, to be tough. I don't remember how it started, this longing for toughness. Perhaps it was our approaching but undreamed of puberty. Or the ebbing of parental supervision and certain possibilities of freedom that went with it.

Roberta was a dreamy girl who loved animals better than human beings; she had seen *Bambi* seven times and always was drawing pictures of spotted fawns. JoAnn Brown was short and wiry and wore glasses, and could stand any amount of pain; the winter before she had been hospitalized with double pneumonia. *Double pneumonia.* "But I had the will to live," she told us solemnly. The three of us were invited to play commandoes with the boys on the block, and once the commando leader, Terry Shea, told another boy, in my hearing, that for a girl I was tough as nails. *Tough as nails.* It did not seem wildly improbable to JoAnn and Roberta and me that we should be the capturers of the crazed killer. Nancy Drew stalked criminals. Why not us?

In JoAnn Brown's house there was a spare room, and in the spare room there was a closet. That closet became the secret headquarters for the detective club. We had a desk which was a cardboard carton turned upside down, and there, sitting on the floor with Mr. Brown's flashlight and stacks of saltines, we studied all the newspaper clippings we could find. We discussed and theorized. Where did the killer hide out? When and where would he strike again? Always behind our plotting and planning lay certain thoughts of honor and reward, the astonishment of our parents when they discovered that we had been the ones who led the police to the killer's hideout, that we had supplied the missing clue; how amazed they would be, they who all summer supposed that their daughters were merely playing, believing that we were children, girls, that we were powerless.

We emerged from these dark closet meetings dazed with heat and determination, and then we would take to the streets. All that summer we followed suspicious-looking men. Short men. Swarthy men. Men with facial scars or crossed eyes. One day we sighted a small dark man, a dwarf, in fact, carrying over his shoulder a large cloth sack. A body? Perhaps the body of a child? We followed him for an hour, and when he disappeared into an electrical-supply shop, JoAnn made careful note of the address and the time of entry.

Back in the closet we discussed what we should do. Should we send a letter to the police? Or should we make our way back to the shop and keep watch?

Roberta said she would be too frightened to go back.

"Well, I'll go then," I spoke bravely.

Bravely, yes, I spoke with thrilling courage. But the truth

was this: I was for all of that summer desperately ill with fear. The instant I was put to bed at night my second-floor bedroom became a cave of pure sweating terror. Atoms of fear conjoined in a solid wall of darkness, pinning me down as I lay paralyzed in the middle of my bed; even to touch the edges of the mattress would be to invite unspeakable violence. The window, softly curtained with dotted swiss, became the focus of my desperate hour-by-hour attention. If I shut my eyes, even for an instant, he, the killer, the maniac, would seize that moment to enter and stab me through the heart. I could hear the sound of the knife entering my chest, a wet, injurious, cataclysmic plunge.

It was the same every night; leaves playing on the window pane, adumbration, darkness, the swift transition from neighborhood heroine, the girl known to be tough as nails, the girl who was on the trail of a murderer, to this, this shallow-breathing, rigidly sleepless coward.

Every night my mother, cheerful, baffled, innocent as she said good night, would remark, "Beats me how you can sleep in a room with the window closed." Proving how removed she was from my state of suffering, how little she perceived my nightly ordeal.

I so easily could have told her that I was afraid. She would have understood; she would have rocked me in her arms, bought me a night light at Woolworth's, explained how groundless my fears really were; she would have poured assurance and comfort on me and, ironically, I knew her comfort would have brought release.

But it was comfort I couldn't afford. At the risk of my life I had to go on as I was, to confess fear to anyone at all would have been to surrender the tough new self that had begun to grow inside me, the self I had created and now couldn't do without.

Then, almost accidentally, I was rescued. It was not my mother who rescued me, but my old doll, Nancy Lynn. I had a glimpse of her one morning in my closet, a plaster arm poking out at me. I pulled her down. She still wore the lacy bonnet on her chipped head, gray with dirt, the ribbons shredded. She had no clothes, only her soft, soiled, mattressy body and the flattened joints where the arms and legs were attached. After all these years her eyes still opened and shut, and her eyelids were a bright youthful pink in contrast to the darkened skin tone of her face.

That night she slept with me under the sheet and malevolence drained like magic from the darkened room; the night pressed friendly and familiar through the dotted swiss curtains; the Callahans' fox terrier yapped at the streaky moon. I opened the window and could hear a breeze loosened in the elms. In bed, Nancy Lynn's cold plaster toe poked reassuringly at my side. Her cloth body, with its soiled cottony fragrance, lay against my bare arm. The powerful pink eyelids were inexpressibly at rest. All night, while I slept, she kept me alive.

For as long as I needed her — I don't remember whether it was weeks or months before the killer was caught — she guarded me at night. The detective club became over a period of time a Gene Autry Fan Club, then a Perry Como Record Club, and there must have been a day when Nancy Lynn went back to her closet. And probably, though I don't like to think of it, a day when she and the others fell victim to a particularly heavy spree of spring cleaning.

There seems no sense to it. Even on the night I first put her on the pillow beside me, I knew she was lifeless, knew there was no heart fluttering in her soft chest and no bravery in her hollow head. None of it was real, none of it.

Only her power to protect me. Human love, I saw, could not always be relied upon. There would be times when I would have to settle for a kind of parallel love, an extension of my hidden self, hidden even from me. It would have to do, it would be a great deal better than nothing, I saw. It was something to be thankful for.

Invitations

ON MONDAY she looked in her mailbox, although she had no reason to expect a letter so soon. But there it was, a small, square card. She held it in her two hands, testing its weight.

It was an invitation to an exhibition of drawings at a private gallery. The name of the artist was only faintly familiar to her, and she couldn't decide if she'd ever seen his work or not. She tried to imagine what kind of drawings she was being invited to view — would they be primitive or abstract or what was sometimes called "magic realism"? She summoned these categories to mind and then decided it didn't matter. What mattered was that she had been invited.

The invitation pleased her, though she wasn't such a fool as to think she'd been specifically singled out because of her aesthetic sensitivity or because of her knowledge of modern graphics or even because of the pleasure of her company. The address on the card had been typed; her name, in fact, was misspelled, the last two letters transposed. Somewhere, no doubt, she'd turned up on a mailing list — that was all.

She would wear a certain printed velvet skirt she had and with it a black turtleneck sweater. No one would expect her to buy a drawing or even to comment on the exhibition. It was necessary only to accept a glass of wine and a cube of orange cheese and stand for a minute or two in front of each drawing, nodding comprehendingly and perhaps murmuring something properly neutral into the air such as "nicely detailed" or "wonderful sense of space." There was a good chance no one would even speak to her, but it would be better than spending Saturday evening in her new apartment, sitting in an armchair with a book and feeling loneliness drink her drop by drop.

The previous tenant had left behind a single item, which was a paperback copy of Jane Austen's *Mansfield Park*, a book that, oddly enough, she had always intended to read. She couldn't help feeling there had been something deliberate — and something imperative, too — about this abandoned book, as though it had been specifically intended for her and that she was being enjoined to take it seriously. But how much better it would be to be going *out*; how much easier it would be to say, should anyone ask, that on Saturday evening she would be attending an opening of an interesting new exhibition.

On Tuesday she was again taken by surprise, for in her mailbox there was another invitation, this time for a cocktail party given by a distant friend of a friend, someone she'd never met but whose name she dimly remembered having heard. It was a disappointment that the party was being held on the same night as the gallery opening and that, furthermore, it was at the same hour. For a minute she entertained the possibility of attending both functions, galloping breathlessly from one to the other. But no, it was not feasible; the two parties were at opposite ends of the city. It was a great pity, she felt, since invitations are few and far between when one moves to a new address. She would have to make a choice.

Of course she would choose the cocktail party. The gallery opening, now that she stopped to think about it, was no more than a commercial venture, an enticement to buyers and patrons. It would be fraudulent of her to attend when she'd no intention of buying a picture, and besides, she was drawn to cocktail parties. She was attracted, in fact, to parties of all kinds, seeing them as an opportunity to possess, for a few hours at least, a life that was denser, more concentrated and more vigorous than the usual spun-out wastes of time that had to be scratched endlessly for substance. She could still wear her certain velvet skirt, but with a pretty red satin blouse she'd recently acquired.

On Wednesday, strangely, she received a third invitation — and it, too, was for Saturday evening. This time the invitation was handwritten, a rather charming note which she read through quickly three times. She was being invited to a small buffet supper. There would be only a dozen or so guests, it was explained. The author of a new biography would be there, and so would the subject of the biography who was, by chance, also a biographer. A particular balding computer scientist would be in attendance along with his wife, who was celebrated for her anti-nuclear stance and for her involvement in Navajo rugs. There would be a professor of history and also a professor of histology, as well as a person renowned for his love of Black Forest cakes and cheese pastries. There would be a famous character actor whose face was familiar, if not his name, and also the hairdresser who'd invented the Gidget cut and raised razor cuts to their present *haute* status.

Of course she could not say no. How much more congenial to go to a supper party than to peer at violent works of art and mutter, "Interesting, interesting," and how much more rewarding than standing about with a drink and a salty canapé and trying to make conversation with a room full of strangers. Her green silk dress would be suitable, if not precisely perfect, and she could gamble safely enough on the fact that no one would have seen it before.

Thursday's mail brought still another invitation, also unfortunately for Saturday evening. She smiled, remembering how her mother used to say, "It never rains but it pours." The invitation, which was for a formal dinner party, was printed on fine paper, and there was a handwritten note at the bottom. "We do hope you can make it," the note said. "Of course we know you by reputation and we've been looking forward to meeting you for years."

It had been some time since she'd attended a formal dinner party, and she was flattered to be sent an invitation with a handwritten note at the bottom. It pleased her to imagine a large, vaulted dining room and parade of courses elegantly served, each with a different wine. The gleam of light through cut glass would sparkle on polished linen and on the faces of the luminaries gathered around the table. Her green silk, with perhaps the double strand of pearls, would be festive enough, but at the same time subdued and formal.

She wasn't entirely surprised to look into her mailbox on Friday and see that she'd been sent yet another invitation. The paper was a heavy, creamy stock and came enclosed in a thick double envelope. There was to be a reception — a *gala* it was called — at the top of a large downtown hotel on Saturday evening. The guest of honor, she read, was to be herself.

She felt a lurch of happiness. Such an honor! But a moment later her euphoria gave way to panic, and when she sat down to collect herself, she discovered she was trembling not with excitement but with fear.

On Saturday she surveyed the five invitations which were arranged in a circle on her coffee table. These missives, so richly welcoming, persuading and honoring, had pleased her at first, then puzzled her. And now she felt for the first time directly threatened. Something or someone was conspiring to consume a portion of her life, of herself, in fact — entering her apartment and taking possesion of her Saturday evening just as a thief might enter and carry off her stereo equipment or her lovely double rope of pearls or a deep slice of her dorsal flesh.

She decided to stay home instead with a cup of coffee and her adventitiously acquired copy of *Mansfield Park*. Already it was dark, and she switched on the small reading lamp by her chair. The shade of the lamp was made of a pale, ivory-yellow material, and the light that shone through it had the warm quality of very old gold.

It happened that people passing her window on their way to various parties and public gatherings that night were moved to see her, a woman sitting calmly in an arc of lamplight, turning over — one by one — the soft pages of a thick book. Clearly she was lost in what she was reading, for she never once glanced up. Her look of solitary containment and the oblique angle with which the light struck the left side of her face made her seem piercingly lovely. One of her hands, curved like a comma, lay on her lap; the other, slowly, thoughtfully, turned over the pages.

Those who passed by and saw her were seized by a twist of pain, which was really a kind of nostalgia for their childhood and for a simplified time when they, too, had been bonded to the books they read and to certain golden rooms which they remembered as being complete and as perfect as stage settings. They felt resentment, too, at the cold rain and the buffeting wind and the price of taxis and the hostility of their hosts. They felt embarrassed by their own small, proffered utterances and by the expanded social rubric they had come to inhabit.

As they moved to and fro in large, brightly-lit rooms, so high up in glittering towers that they felt they were clinging to the sides of cliffs, their feet began to ache and exhaustion overcame them. Soon it was past midnight, no longer the same day, but the next and the next. New widths of time clamored to be filled, though something it seemed, some image of possibility, begged to be remembered.

Outside, the wind blew and blew. The sky slipped sideways, turning first yellow, then a mournful, treasonous purple, as though time itself was drowning in a waterfall of shame.

Taking the Train

GWENETH McGOWAN, the Disraeli scholar, was awarded the Saul Appeldorf Medal at a gala reception. She carried it home and put it in a dresser drawer under a pile of underwear. Her morale was high. Recognition in the academic world seemed assured, her rent was paid up for six months and, in addition, she had a number of good friends, some deserving of her friendship, and some not.

"Dear Gweneth," came a letter from Calgary, Alberta where one of the deserving friends lived. "So! Now you're famous! Well, well. Why not treat yourself to a visit — come and see me."

Within a week Gweneth was on a plane. Northie McCord, her friend and former roommate at school, met her at the airport with a bouquet of daisies. "Ah, daisies," Gweneth said without amazement. Memory was the first bag they reached into on their infrequent meetings, and Northie's offering of daisies was meant to dislodge and recover images of her wedding day when bride and bridesmaids, Gweneth included, had worn crowns of daisies on their heads. They also had worn peace buttons pinned to their smooth silk bodices.

"Just who the hell did we think we were?" Northie asked Gweneth later that day when the two of them were settled on canvas chairs in Northie's untidy backyard. "Who exactly did we think we were performing for?"

She passed Gweneth what was left of a joint. "I don't know about you, but I think I was trying to say I hadn't capitulated just because I was marrying a chemical engineer. What I should have said was that I was damn well ready to capitulate."

"We were tired," said Gweneth, who had no recollection of being tired, but wasn't ready yet to talk about Northie's husband, who had been mauled to death by a grizzly in a provincial park the year before. (According to a news report in an eastern paper, the attack had been "provoked" by the ham sandwich he carried in the pocket of his jacket; such an innocent act, Gweneth had thought at the time, to carry a ham sandwich.)

"A remarkable sky", she said to Northie, and the two of them fell into a loop of silence that only very old friends can enter easily.

There had been a period of several years when they'd been out of touch. In those years Gweneth was working on a Ph.D. and, for the most part, was without money. Being without money made her wayward, and waywardness permitted her a series of small abdications: letters, phone calls, reunions — they all went by the board. Sometimes, too, she lacked courage. "I don't have anything to show!" she confessed to an early lover, not sure whether she meant silverware or children or that hard lacquer she thought of as happiness. Later, she came to see happiness as something chancy and unreliable, a flash of light beating at the edge of a human eye or a thin piece of glass to be carried secretly inside her head.

Northie McCord's fifteen-year-old daughter, also named Gweneth but called Gwen for short, was excited by Gweneth's visit and insisted on making supper for the three of them. On a card table on the back porch she set out cold sliced beef, potato salad from a carton and glasses of iced tea.

Along with the cold beef there was a ceramic pot of fiery mustard. "Superb," Gweneth pronounced as her mouth filled with splendid heat. "Wherever did you get such wonderful stuff?"

Northie and her daughter exchanged sly smiles. "It's our own," Northie said. "Didn't you notice those mustard plants in the yard?"

Gweneth helped herself to more beef and mustard. "God

forgive me, I thought it was weeds." She felt for a moment that rare sensation of stepping outside her body and entering a narrative that belonged not to any one of them, but that was shared equally.

After supper, Gwen washed the dishes and Northie led Gweneth over to the cedar fence where there was a double row of mustard plants. There are two types, Northie explained, black and white, and the best mustard in the world is made by combining the two.

"I didn't know what to do with myself last winter," Northie said, "but I remembered how you read right through Carthusian-to-Crockroft when you were seventeen. What was it? — volume four of the encyclopedia?"

"Volume five. If I remember, I was troubled by my virginity and looked up *coitus* one day, and then just buried myself in all those lovely C's. That's how I discovered John Clare and that led me to the nineteenth century and that led to Disraeli."

"I settled down with volume fifteen," Northie said, "maybe because Gwen was fifteen. Maximinus-to-Naples, that's what volume fifteen is called. Maximinus, in case you're wondering, was one of the Roman emperors. About February I got to *mustard*. According to the encyclopedia, mustard grows plentifully in Montana, and so I thought, well, why not in Alberta? I had a devil of a time getting the right seedlings. You can cook the greens, too, if you rinse them twice, but I thought I'd better not inflict that on you."

She bent down to pick a leaf for Gweneth, and when she stood up her eyes were filled with tears. "It's a diversion," she said. "It's something to show people when they drop in."

"You are," Gweneth said loudly, hugging her, "the most successful mustard farmer I've ever met."

The girl, Gwen, flushed from the heat of the kitchen, carried two cups of coffee into the yard. "For McCord and McGowan," she said, and dropped a mock curtsy.

"We sound like sweater manufacturers."

"Or quality chocolates."

The two women moved the lawn chairs into a last remaining

patch of sun and sat talking about the past, about what they had been like as girls of sixteen and seventeen. They'd done this before, but it seemed to Gweneth that they'd never done it so thoroughly — it was as though they were obliged, for the sake of the future, to rescue every moment. She remembered what one of her lovers had said: "What is the point of nostalgia if not to wring memory dry."

The evening grew chilly. A breeze came up, and Gweneth swore she could smell mustard in the air. Gwen brought them more coffee, a cardigan for her mother and a lacy wool shawl for Gweneth. "She's playing handmaiden tonight," Northie said when the girl had gone back into the house to her Bruce Springsteen records. "She's got very maternal since Mac was killed. She thinks this is what I need, to sit and talk with an old friend."

Gweneth asked, "And is it what you need?"

"Yes," Northie said. "But I don't need to talk about *it*. You don't want that, and I can't quite manage it."

"It isn't a question of my wanting it or not wanting it. If you want to talk, well, that's —"

"That's what you came for?"

"I was going to say that, but it's not true, of course. I don't think comfort is what you and I are able to do for each other. It wasn't in our syllabus, as the saying goes."

"The night before Mac left for that hiking trip we sat out here. Just like tonight. Except, the most extraordinary thing happened. There was a display of northern lights — have you ever seen the northern lights?"

Gweneth said no, glad she could say no.

"It's rather rare just here. Normally, you have to be away from the city because the general illumination interferes. But something was just right with the atmosphere that night, and it was a dazzling show. I hadn't imagined it would be so precisely outlined as it's shown in pictures — those folded curtains dragging down from the heavens. Mac said — I remember his exact words — he said all we needed was a celestial choir.

Straight out of MGM, corny as hell. You know I'm not one for omens and portents, but it's given me something to hang on to. Along with Maximinus and mustard. And Gwen, of course.''

"You're lucky to have a child. That's something I'm sorry I missed." Gweneth said this even though it wasn't true. (The lie didn't bother her at all since she knew it did people good to be fulsomely envied.) She had never wished for a child. Once she said to a man she was living with, "The saddest thing in the world is a woman who thinks with her womb." "No," he said, "the saddest thing in the world is an artist whose work speaks to no one." This man, an abstract painter by profession, was always watering down her observations, and eventually it drove her straight into the arms of a Guggenheim Fellowship.

When her thesis was published, she liked to pat its brown covers and say, "Hi there, baby." When she was interviewed, shaking, on the BBC — the Third Programme yet — she found herself talking about her research like a mother, and indulging in a mother's fond praising, defensive and fault-finding by turn. And once she sat in the Reading Room of the British Museum and examined a tiny nineteenth-century book of essays written by an obscure country clergyman. The binding had long since deteriorated, and the pages had been tied together by someone — who? — when? — with a piece of ribbon. Slowly, respectfully, she'd tried to undo the knot, but the ribbon was so stiff with age that it crumbled on the table into a kind of white powder. She had examined the severed pages with more tenderness and sense of privilege than she'd ever felt toward anything in her life, and it occurred to her that perhaps this is what mothers feel for the secret lives of their children. Surely — she glanced at Northie — such moments keep people from flying into pieces.

"I didn't know you ever wanted children," Northie said after a while. "I mean, you never said."

They sat in silence a little longer until they began to shiver with cold.

When they came into the house, they found Gwen sitting on

the living-room floor listening to a Bruce Springsteen record, a long moaning song. She held up the record sleeve, which said: "New York City Serenade."

"It's coming," she told the two of them as they stood in the doorway. "The best part is coming." She shut her eyes and held up a finger, just as the song changed abruptly from gravel-weighted melody to anguished wail and the repeated phrase, "'She won't take the train, she won't take the train.'" Listening, her face went luminous with sorrow and her lips mouthed the tragic words. "'No, she won't take the train, no, she won't take the train.'"

Who won't take the train? Gweneth wanted to demand roughly. Why not? And did it matter? The mystery was that a phrase so rich with denial could enthrall a young girl.

Gweneth felt an impulse to rescue her with logic, with exuberance, but stopped just in time. An image came into her mind, an old, traditional image of women who, after a meal, will take a tablecloth, shake it free of crumbs and put it away, each taking a corner, folding it once, then twice, then again. They never hesitate, these women, moving in and out, in and out, as skilled and graceful as dancers. And now, Gweneth thought: here we are, the three of us, holding on to this wailing rag-tag of music for all we're worth, and to something else that we can't put a name to, but don't dare drop.

Home

IT WAS SUMMER, the middle of July, the middle of this century, and in the city of Toronto 100 people were boarding an airplane.

"Right this way," the lipsticked stewardess cried. "Can I get you a pillow? A blanket?"

It was a fine evening, and they climbed aboard with a lightsome step, even those who were no longer young. The plane was on its way to London, England, and since this was before the era of jet aircraft, a transatlantic flight meant twelve hours in the air. Ed Dover, a man in his mid-fifties who worked for the Post Office, had cashed in his war bonds so that he and his wife, Barbara, could go back to England for a twenty-one-day visit. It was for Barbara's sake they were going; the doctor had advised it. For two years she had suffered from depression, forever talking about England and the village near Braintree where she had grown up and where her parents still lived. At home in Toronto she sat all day in dark corners of the house, helplessly weeping; there was dust everywhere, and the little back garden where rhubarb and raspberries had thrived was overtaken by weeds.

Ed had tried to cheer her first with optimism, then with presents — a television set, a Singer sewing machine, boxes of candy. But she talked only about the long, pale Essex twilight, or a remembered bakeshop in the High Street, or sardines on toast around the fire, or the spiky multicolored lupins that bloomed by the back door. If only she could get lupins to grow in Toronto, things might be better.

Ed and Barbara now sat side by side over a wing, watching

the propellers warm up. She looked out the window and dozed. It seemed to her that the sky they traveled through was sliding around the earth with them, given thrust by the fading of the sun's color. She thought of the doorway of her parents' house, the green painted gate and the stone gateposts that her father polished on Saturday mornings.

Then, at the same moment, and for no reason, the thought of this English house fused perfectly with the image of her own house, hers and Ed's, off Keele Street in Toronto, how snug it was in winter with the new fitted carpet and the work Ed had done in the kitchen, and she wondered suddenly why she'd been so unhappy there. She felt something like a vein reopening in her body, a flood of balance restored, and when the stewardess came around with the supper tray, Barbara smiled up at her and said, "Why, that looks fit for a king."

Ed plunged into his dinner with a good appetite. There was duckling with orange sauce and, though he wasn't one for fancy food, he always was willing to try something new. He took one bite and then another. It had a sweet, burned taste, not unpleasant, which for some reason reminded him of the sharpness and strangeness of sexual desire, the way it came uninvited at queer moments — when he was standing in the bathroom shaving his cheeks, or when he hurried across Eglinton Avenue in the morning to catch his bus. It rose bewilderingly like a spray of fireworks, a fountain that was always brighter than he remembered, going on from minute to minute, throwing sparks into the air and out onto the coolness of grass. He remembered, too, something almost forgotten: the smell of Barbara's skin when she stepped out of the bath and, remembering, felt the last two years collapse softly into a clock tick, their long anguish becoming something he soon would be looking back upon. His limbs seemed light as a boy's. The war bonds, their value badly nibbled away by inflation, had been well-exchanged for this moment of bodily lightness. Let it come, let it come, he said to himself, meaning the rest of his life.

Across from Ed and Barbara, a retired farmer from Rivers,

Manitoba sat chewing his braised duckling. He poked his wife in the knees and said, "For God's sake, for God's sake," referring, in his withered tenor voice, to the exotic meal and also to the surpassing pleasure of floating in the sky at nine o'clock on a fine summer evening with first Quebec, then the wide ocean skimming beneath him.

His wife was not a woman who appreciated being poked in the knees, but she was too busy thinking about God and Jesus and loving mercy and the color of the northern sky, which was salmon shading into violet, to take offense. She sent the old man, her husband for forty years, a girlish, new-minted smile, then brought her knuckles together and marveled at the sliding terraces of grained skin covering the backs of her hands. Sweet Jesus our Savior — the words went off inside her ferny head like popcorn.

Not far from her sat a journalist, a mole-faced man with a rounded back, who specialized in writing profiles of the famous. He went around the world phoning them, writing to them, setting up appointments with them, meeting them in hotels or in their private quarters to spy out their inadequacies, their tragedies, their blurted fears, so that he could then treat them — and himself — to lavish bouts of pity. It was hard work, for the personalities of the famous vanish into their works, but always, after one of his interviews, he was able to persuade himself that it was better, when all was said and done, to be a nobody. In Canada he had interviewed the premier of a large eastern province, a man who had a gray front tooth, a nervous tremor high up on one cheek and a son-in-law who was about to go to jail for a narcotics offense. Now the journalist was going home to his flat in Notting Hill Gate; in twenty-four hours he would be fingering his collection of tiny glass animals and thinking that, despite his relative anonymity, his relative loneliness, his relatively small income and the relatively scanty degree of recognition that had come his way — despite this, his prized core of neutrality was safe from invaders. And what did that mean? — he asked himself this with the same winning interrogation he practised on the famous. It meant happiness, or something akin to happiness.

Next to him sat a high school English teacher, a woman of forty-odd years, padded with soft fat and dressed in a stiff shantung travel suit. Once in England, she intended to take a train to the Lake District and make her way to Dove Cottage where she would sign her name in the visitors' book as countless other high school teachers had done. When she returned to Toronto, a city in which she had never felt at home, though she'd been born there, and when she went back to her classroom in September to face unmannerly adolescents who would never understand what *The Prelude* was about, it would be a comfort for her to think of her name inscribed in a large book on a heavy oak table — as she imagined it — in the house where William Wordsworth had actually lived. The world, she suddenly saw, was accessible; oceans and continents and centuries could be spryly overleapt. From infancy she'd been drawn toward those things that were transparent — glass, air, rain, even the swimmy underwaterness of poetry. The atmosphere on the plane, its clear chiming ozone, seemed her true element, rarified, tender, discovered. Thinking this, she put back her head and heard the pleasurable crinkle of her new perm, a crinkle that promised her safe passage — or anything else she desired or could imagine.

They all were happy, Ed and Barbara Dover, the lip-smacking farmer and his prayerful wife, the English journalist, and the Toronto teacher — but they were far from being the only ones. By some extraordinary coincidence (or cosmic dispensation or whatever), each person on the London-bound flight that night was, for a moment, filled with the steam of perfect happiness. Whether it was the oxygen-enriched air of the fusiform cabin, or the duckling with orange sauce, or the soufflé-soft buttocks of the stewardess sashaying to and fro with her coffeepot, or the unchartable currents of air bouncing against the sides of the vessel, or some random thought dredged out of the darkness of the aircraft and fueled by the proximity of strangers — whatever it was, each of the 100 passengers — one after another, from rows one to twenty-five, like little lights going on —

experienced an intense, simultaneous sensation of joy. They were for that moment swimmers riding a single wave, tossed upwards by infection or clairvoyance or a slant of perception uniquely heightened by an accident of altitude.

Even the pilot, a Captain Walter Woodlock, a man plagued by the most painful and chronic variety of stomach ulcers, closed his eyes for the briefest of moments over Greenland and drifted straight into a fragment of dream. It couldn't have lasted more than thirty seconds, but in that short time he felt himself falling into a shrug of relaxation he'd almost forgotten. Afloat in his airy dimension, he became a large wet rose nodding in a garden, a gleaming fish smiling on a platter, a thick slice of Arctic moon reaching down and tenderly touching the small uplifted salty waves. He felt he could go on drifting forever in this false loop of time, so big and so blue was the world at that moment.

It must have been that the intensity and heat of this gathered happiness produced a sort of gas or ether or alchemic reaction — it's difficult to be precise — but for a moment, perhaps two, the walls of the aircraft, the entire fuselage and wings and tail section became translucent. The layers of steel, the rivets and bracing and ribwork turned first purple, then a pearly pink, and finally metamorphosed to the incandescence of pure light.

This luminous transformation, needless to say, went unnoticed by those in the aircraft, so busy was each of them with his or her private vision of transcendence.

But there was, it turned out, one witness: a twelve-year-old boy who happened to be standing on a stony Greenland beach that midsummer night. His name was Piers and he was the son of a Danish Lutheran clergyman who had come to the tiny Greenland village for a two-year stint. The boy's mother had remained behind in Copenhagen, having fallen in love with a manufacturer of pharmaceuticals, and none of this had been adequately explained to the boy — which may have been why he was standing, lonely and desperately confused, on the barren beach so late at night.

It was not very dark, of course. In Greenland, in the middle of the summer, the sky keeps some of its color until eleven o'clock, and even after that there are traces of brightness, much like the light that adheres to small impurities suspended in wine. The boy heard the noise of the motors first, looked up frowningly and saw the plane, shiningly present with its chambered belly and elegant glassy wings and the propellers spinning their milky webs. He was too dazzled to wave, which was what he normally did when a plane passed overhead. What could it be? he asked himself. He knew almost nothing of science fiction, a genre scorned by his father, and the church in which he had been reared strictly eschewed angelic hosts or other forms of bodily revelation. A trick of the atmosphere? — he had already seen the aurora borealis and knew this was different. The word *phenomenon* had not yet entered his vocabulary, but when it did, a few years later, dropping like a ripe piece of fruit into his consciousness, he found that it could usefully contain something of the spectacle of that night.

Such moments of intoxication, of course, quickly become guilty secrets — this is especially true of children — so it is not surprising that he never told anyone about what he had seen.

Like his father, he grew up to become a man of God, though like others of his generation he wore the label with irony. He went first to Leiden to study, and there lost his belief in the Trinity. After that he received a fellowship to the Union Theological Seminary in New York where his disbelief grew, as did his reputation for being a promising young theologian. Before long he was invited to join the faculty; he became, in a few short years, the author of a textbook and a sought-after lecturer, and in his late thirties he fell in love with a nervous, intelligent woman who was a scholar of medieval history.

One night, when wrapped in each other's arms, she told him how women in the Middle Ages had pulled their silk gowns through a golden ring to test the fineness of the cloth. It seemed to him that this was the way in which he tested his belief in God, except that instead of determining the fineness of faith, he charted its reluctance, its lumpiness, its ultimate absurdity. Nevertheless, against all odds, there were days when he was able to pull what little he possessed through the ring; it came out with a ripply whoosh of surprise, making him feel faint and bringing instantly to mind the image of the transparent airplane suspended in the sky of his childhood. All his life seemed to him to have been a centrifugal voyage around that remembered vision — the only sign of mystery he had ever received.

One day, his limbs around his beloved and his brain burning with pleasure, he told her what he had once been privileged to see. She pulled away from him then — she was a woman with cool eyes and a listening mouth — and suggested he see a psychiatrist.

Thereafter, he saw less and less of her, and finally, a year later, a friend told him she had married someone else. The same friend suggested he should take a holiday.

It was summertime, the city was sweltering, and it had been some time since he had been able to pull anything at all through his gold ring. He considered returning to Greenland for a visit, but the flight schedule was unbelievably complicated and the cost prohibitive; only wealthy birdwatchers working on their life lists could afford to go there now. He found himself one afternoon in a travel agent's office next to a pretty girl who was booking a flight to Acapulco.

"Fabulous place," she said. Glorious sun. Great beaches. And grass by the bushel.

Always before, when the frivolous, leisured world beckoned, he had solemnly refused. But now he bought himself a ticket, and by the next morning he was on his way.

At the airport in Acapulco, a raw duplicity hangs in the blossom-sweet air — or so thinks Josephe, a young woman who works as a baggage checker behind the customs desk. All day long fresh streams of tourists arrive. From her station she can see them stepping off their aircraft and pressing forward through the wide glass doors, carrying with them the conspiratorial heft of vacationers-on-the-move. Their soft-sided luggage, their tennis rackets, their New York pallor and anxious brows expose in Josephe a buried vein of sadness, and one day she notices something frightening; 109 passengers step off the New York plane, and each of them — without exception — is wearing blue jeans.

She's used to the sight of blue jeans, but such statistical unanimity is unnerving, as though a comic army has grotesquely intruded. Even the last passenger to disembark and step onto the tarmac, a man who walks with the hesitant gait of someone in love with his own thoughts, is wearing the ubiquitous blue jeans.

She wishes there had been a single exception — a woman in a bright flowered dress or a man archaic enough to believe that resort apparel meant white duck trousers. She feels oddly assaulted by such totality, but the feeling quickly gives way to a head-shaking thrill of disbelief, then amusement, then satisfaction and, finally, awe.

She tries hard to get a good look at the last passenger's face, the one who sealed the effect of unreality, but the other passengers crowd around her desk, momentarily threatened by her small discoveries and queries, her transitory power.

In no time it's over; the tourists, duly processed, hurry out into the sun. They feel lighter than air, they claim, freer than birds, drifting off into their various inventions of paradise as though oblivious to the million invisible filaments of connection, trivial or profound, which bind them one to the other and to the small green planet they call home.

The Journal

WHEN HAROLD AND SALLY TRAVEL, Sally keeps a journal, and in this journal Harold becomes *H*. She will write down such things as "H. exclaimed how the cathedral (Reims) is melting away on the outside and eroding into abstract lumps — while the interior is all fluidity and smoothness and grace, a seemingly endless series of rising and arching."

Has Harold actually *exclaimed* any such thing? The phrase *seemingly endless* sounds out of character, a little spongy, in fact, but then people sometimes take on a different persona when they travel. The bundled luggage, the weight of the camera around the neck, the sheer cost of air fare make travelers eager to mill expansive commentary from minor observation. Sally, in her journal, employs a steady, marching syntax, but allows herself occassional forays into fancy.

Both Harold and Sally are forty years old, the parents of two young children, boys. Harold possesses a mild, knobby face — his father was Swedish, his mother Welsh — and the natural dignity of one who says less than he feels. After he and his wife, Sally, leave the cathedral, they walk back to the Hotel du Nord where they are staying, down one of those narrow, busy streets which the French like to describe as *bien animé*, and everywhere, despite a thick mist of rain, people are busy coming and going. Since it is close to five o'clock, they're beginning to gather in small cafés and bars and *salons du thé* in order to treat themselves to glasses of wine or beer or perhaps small cups of bitter espresso. A *quotidian quaff* is the tickling phrase that pops into Harold's head, and it seems to him there is not one person in all of Reims, in all of France for that matter, who is not now happily seated in some warm public corner and raising pleasing liquids to his lips. He experiences a nudge of grief because he does not happen to live in a country where people gather publicly at this hour to sip drinks and share anecdotes and debate ideas. He and Sally live on the fringe of Oshawa, Ontario where, at the end of the working day, people simply return to their homes and begin to prepare their evening meal as though lacking the imagination to think of more joyous activities. But here, at a little table in France, the two of them have already gone native — "H. and I have gone native..." — and sit sipping cups of tea and eating little pancakes sprinkled with sugar. Harold feels inexpressibly at peace — which makes him all the more resentful that he can't live the rest of his life in this manner, but he decides against mentioning his ambivalent feelings to Sally for fear she'll write them down in her journal. ("H. laments the sterility of North American life which insists on the isolation of the family rather than the daily ceremony of...")

The Hotel du Nord is much like other provincial hotels in its price bracket, possessing as it does a certain dimness of light bulbs, rosy wallpaper printed with medallions, endless creaking corridors lined with numbered doors and, especially, a proprietor's young brown-eyed son who sits in the foyer at a little table doing his homework, his *devoir* as he calls it. It's a lesson on the configuration of the Alps that occupies this young boy and keeps his smooth dark head bent low. The angle of the boy's bent neck sharpens Harold's sorrow, which has been building since he and Sally left the cathedral. ("H. was deeply moved by the sight of...")

Their room is small, the bed high and narrow and the padded satin coverlet not quite clean. Between coarse white sheets they attempt to make love, and almost, but not quite, succeed. Neither blames the other. Sally curses the remnant of jet lag and Harold suspects the heaviness of the bedcovers; at home they've grown used to the lightness of a single electric blanket. But the tall shutters at the Hotel du Nord keep the little room

wonderfully, profoundly, dark, and the next morning Harold
remarks that there's probably a market in Canada for
moveable shutters instead of the merely decorative Colonial
type. ("H. has become an enthusiastic advocate of . . .")

It seems that the hotel, despite its great number of rooms,
is almost empty. At least there is only one other guest having
breakfast with Sally and Harold the next morning, a young
man sitting at the table next to theirs, drinking his coffee
noisily and nibbling a bun. Out of pity — for the young, for
the solitary — they engage him in conversation. He's an
Australian, hungry for cricket scores, scornful of New
Zealanders, and illiterate in French — altogether a dull young
man; there's no other word for it. ("What a waste, H. says,
to come so far and be so dull!!")

Rain, rain, rain. To cheer themselves up, Sally and Harold
drive their rented Peugeot to Dijon and treat themselves to
a grand lunch at an ancient *auberge*. ("Awnings, white
tablecloths, the whole ball of wax.") Sally starts with a lovely
and strange salad of warm bacon, chicken livers, tomatoes,
lettuce and parsley. Then something called *Truit Caprice*.
When she chews, an earnest net of wrinkles flies into her
face, and Harold finds this so endearing that he reaches for
her hand. ("H. had the alternate menu — herring — which
may be the cause of his malaise!")

Sunshine, at last, after days of rain, and Sally and Harold
arrive at the tall gates of a château called Rochepot, which
their *Guide Michelin* has not awarded the decency of a single
star. Why not? they wonder aloud.

Because it is largely a restoration, their tour guide says.
She's middle-aged, with a broad fused bosom, and wears an
apron over her green wool suit. Stars, she says, are reserved for
those things that are authentic. Nevertheless, the château is
spectacular with its patterned roofs and pretty interior garden
— and Sally and Harold, after the rain, after yet another night
of sexual failure, are anxious to appreciate. The circular
château bedchambers are filled with curious hangings, the wide
flagged kitchen is a museum of polished vessels and amusing

contrivances, but what captures Harold's imagination is a little plaque on the garden wall. It shows a picture of a giraffe, and with it goes a brief legend. It seems that the King of Egypt gave the giraffe to the King of France in the year 1827, and that this creature was led, wearing a cloak to keep it from the chill, through the village of Rochepot where it was regarded by all and sundry as a great spectacle. Harold loves the nineteenth century, which he sees as an exuberant epoch that produced and embraced the person he would like to have been: gentleman, generalist, amateur naturalist, calm but skeptical observer of kingships, comets and constellations, of flora and fauna and humanistic philosophy, and at times he can scarcely understand how he's come to be a supervisor in the public school system on the continent of North America. ("H. despairs because...")

In Le Grand Hotel in Beaune, in a second-floor room that faces onto the rue Principal and which is directly accessible all night long to the river of loud traffic destined for the south, Sally and Harold achieve one of those rare moments of sexual extravagance that arrives as a gift perhaps two or three times in one's life. Whether it was an enabling exhaustion — exhaustion can be cumulative, as all travelers know — or whether it was the bottle of soft, pale-red dinner wine — softer than rain, softer even than the sound of the word *rain* — or whether they felt themselves preciously and uniquely abandoned in the strange, many-veined hexagon of France where their children and their children's babysitter and their aged parents and even the Canadian embassy in Paris could not possibly track them down — whatever the reason, they've been led, extraordinarily, into the heaven of ecstasy and then into the cool, air-filled condition of deep rest. Harold sleeps, his eyelids unmoving, and Sally, entering a succession of linked dreams, transcends herself, becoming S., that brave pilgrim on a path of her own devising. The ubiquitous satin coverlet presses and the shutters preserve darkness — though they do next to nothing to keep out the sound of traffic — and the long night leans in on them, blessing the impulse that coaxed them away from Oshawa and from the North American shore into this alien wine-provisioned wilderness where they are minutely and ecstatically joined and where they exchange, as seldom before in their forty-year lives, those perfect notices of affection and trust and rhapsody. ("H. and I slept well and in the morning...")

Salt

HALFWAY THROUGH his Canadian lecture tour, Thornbury found himself at an all-male dinner where the conversation had begun to flag. It seemed to him that much human effort went into separating men from women, and he often wondered why and to what effectiveness. Here, at the — what was it called? The Manitoba Club — there was still a quaint prohibition against women, yet there was something distinctively feminine about the pink-shaded wall lamps and the bowls of wet roses on every table. Women, Thornbury could not help thinking, might have kept the evening livelier; women would not have permitted the sudden falling off of discussion that brings official functions to a self-conscious halt.

This happened between the salad and the dessert course, the final stretch of a small club dinner organized in Thornbury's honor. Politics had been discussed, national and local, and flattering — though vague — references had been made to Thornbury's afternoon lecture. He supposed that, somewhere within his bloated body, his star of celebrity still twinkled, and for that reason he felt an obligation to keep the evening lively. Part of his arrogance, his wife Flora charged, was his belief that he had to assist others over the difficult sill of language. This was not so, he maintained, but he rightly felt that, were it not for his visit, the six men seated at the table would be at home enjoying the company of their wives and children.

Gathered around him were a judge, two lawyers, a deputy provincial minister, the publisher of a small literary quarterly, and a man who had been introduced earlier as a theologian.

Thornbury turned to the theologian, who was sitting on his left, and said, "There's something I've been wondering about lately. It's a biblical question, and perhaps you would be able to provide me with an answer."

At this the theologian looked mildly disoriented, and a bridge of bone over his eyes pushed forward. "Well I'm afraid my Bible's a bit rusty — "

"It's just this," Thornbury said. "Why was it that Lot's wife was turned into a pillar of salt?"

"Disobedience, wasn't it?" The theologian was vague, engagingly so, probing his salad with a busy fork. "She disobeyed God by turning and looking back at the burning city."

"Yes," Thornbury said, "of course. But my question is, why salt? Why not limestone, for instance? Or marble?"

"Salt is soluble," someone pronounced, not very helpfully. One of the lawyers. "Highly perishable, a pillar of salt. Wouldn't last long in this part of the world, not in the springtime anyway."

"But in that part of the world where the rainfall — "

"Didn't Lot's wife have a name?" It was the judge who was speaking, a mild, contemplative man, ridiculously young to be a judge, in Gordon Thornbury's opinion. Earlier, he had predicted that the judge would be the one most likely, as the evening sank beneath the tipping horizon of drink, to address him as *Gord*. (On the Australian tour it had been *Gordo*; in America, once, *Gord-boy*.)

"No woman would stand for it nowadays," the theologian said. "Being labeled Lot's wife, that is. Not my wife, at any rate."

Thornbury felt the conversation drifting off again. This seemed a pattern he had observed elsewhere in North America, the impulse to broaden rather than focus, and he imagined it must have to do with a perceived obligation to democratize even the smallest social discussion. There was something compelling about New World discursiveness, particularly in this flat, pleasant prairie city where the trickle-down despair of the century — like the elm beetle — seemed not to have reached;

this width of fresh faces, this courtesy, this absurd willingness
to offer up an evening from their connubial lives! But he steered
back, nevertheless, to his original question. "Why salt?"
he said again.

The two lawyers scowled as though pretending to think, and
the theologian looked bewildered — in fact, at that moment,
though Thornbury could not have known it, a gas pain shot
across the man's heart, causing him to set down abruptly his
wineglass. A little wine leapt from the glass onto the tablecloth,
a pink stain from which eyes were quickly withdrawn.

The local publisher, springy as an athlete, jumped in with,
"I expect it's an example of metonymy, a term my wife's recently
introduced me to. She would be able to explain it better than I,
but it means that the word *salt*, as used in this case, could
imply a broader catagory — mineral, for instance. Just as,"
he looked around the table, "just as the apple in the story of
Adam and Eve stands for all manner of fruit."

"Hmmmm," said Thornbury, who saw the logic of this but
was reluctant to surrender the image of salt — he was a man
with a gift for selling his private visions to others, and it piqued
him, more than it should, to be diverted.

A number of points were raised. Wasn't salt considered a
luxury? Not in the Mediterranean, where salt was plentiful.
Wasn't salt a preservative? Perhaps Lot's wife was just being
salted away temporarily until she pulled up her socks. (Gruff
laughter here, and Thornbury felt for an instant a chill
maleness breezing off the fairway.) *Was* there, when it came
down to it, such a thing as an actual pillar of salt? The deputy
minister cleared his throat at last and said that, yes, indeed
there was, and that they occurred naturally in underground
caves. It happened that he had been a mining engineer before
entering public life, and he and his wife could vouch for such
curious structures.

"The injustice of it," sighed the youthful judge, not
inappropriately. "Which of us, even Gord here — or our wives
— *wouldn't* have looked back when specifically told not to?
I'm not sure I'd call that disobedience." He shot the theologian
a look. "I'd call it a justifiable compulsion."

"Almost an invitation."

"The gauntlet thrown."

"Absolutely."

"I picture a sort of Ionian column," said the publisher in his speculative way. "With the wind howling around it."

This remark produced a sudden flush of intimacy. "Well," one of the lawyers said, clearly the cleverer one, "what I picture is the female form preserved in the pillar. Like one of those temple goddesses who support the cornices of classical buildings. Last summer my wife and I —"

Thornbury thought of his own wife, Flora, as he had last seen her in London. She was striding away from him at Heathrow, chip-chipping on her high, very slender shoes. He had kissed her lips, something he seldom did in public; she'd been cross with him that day, unexpectedly argumentative and, with some logic, accused him of seizing upon travel as a retreat from difficulty. There was nothing saline about Flora's lips. More like summer fruit, though some would say past ripeness. He recalled the day he first met her. Her hair was a crown of auburn; they had taken a taxi across London, and she had been wearing a rather short skirt which exposed a pair of sharp, carved knees, reminding him, more than anything else, of the small shrewd heads of foxes. His hands had wanted to reach out and cover them.

A week ago, at Heathrow, he'd gone through the barrier and turned for a final look at her, wondering almost abstractly whether she would turn at the same moment. She hadn't. She'd walked briskly to the automatic doors and disappeared. He felt himself stiffen with loneliness. Montreal lay ahead — woods, deep lakes — then Toronto, Winnipeg, Calgary, Vancouver, a stretched follow-the-dot ganglia of effort and rich meals. It was then he thought of Lot's wife, wondering if it had been tears that turned her to salt, her wish to stay rooted in one spot. He was about to risk this thought aloud when he saw that dessert was being served.

Dessert was maple mousse, one of the club specialties, almost always trotted out for foreign guests (or overseas visitors, as the somewhat old-fashioned chef would have put it). In Quebec, Thornbury had been served *jambon au sirop d'érable*, in Toronto a bizarre maple liqueur, and he imagined that, esophagus to gut, he soon would be lined with a bed of sweetness. His health, his celebrity, were toasted with brandy.

"I'm sure you gentlemen will be wanting an early night," he said, acting out of the guilt that attaches to guests of honor and imagining the faithful waiting wives.

It is a trick of perception, he believes, that makes him see these absent wives as faithful. He has absorbed, in the barely glimpsed cities — Melbourne, Perth, Tulsa, Austin, Denver, San Francisco — an impression of marital order, an ongoing pageant celebrating the richness of that phantom, fidelity. A mirage of course. Sweet and druggy, fleeting as music that leaks from car windows, he breathes it in as a necessary potion. "My wife and I" is a phrase he leaps upon. "My wife said to me — " "My wife read your recent article — " These wives, with their unassailable good faith, have won his love. It's they he thinks about before falling asleep in his first-class hotel rooms, though his dreams are about Flora and the helpless worries that gabble behind him like starved geese. He and Flora had once talked about emigrating. Rhodesia was mentioned, he recalls. Well, that would have been a mistake, anyway.

Good night. A pleasure. An honor. Enchanting. Good night. Within minutes, with almost painful haste, the guests scatter, going out through the heavy club doors into a moist spring night. Only the theologian lingers for a moment. His voice is breathy and excited. He intends to pursue the question of Lot's wife, he tells Thornbury. Why salt indeed? An interesting question. No doubt one of the biblical commentaries he has at home will have something to say on the subject. He promises to drop Thornbury a line if he discovers anything.

Thornbury looks at the man's round face, its open, large-eared symmetry and nascent jowls, and clearly sees how he must have looked as an infant, imagining first a fair wisp of hair and then the beginnings of a knitted bonnet with matching satin ribbon bow fixing it to his head. He also divines in him an anxious groping toward recognition — someone in the same boat, as *he* might put it — and even a flimsy uprooted reaching for love. What can he say under the circumstances? Speaking from the heart, Flora always says, turns him to pulp.

He pictures the now inevitable postcard winging its way across the Atlantic, its tough little Canadian stamp and post-mark, its cramped, pedantic printing, the horror of a cheery set of exclamation points, hail-fellow-searcher-after-truth. Dear God.

Flora, elegant and angular, will stoop and pick it up, peer at it and say, slippingly, "What's all *this* about salt?" She cannot imagine his life, what it's composed of and how he conspires to preserve it.

Others

FOR THEIR HONEYMOON, Robert and Lila went to France. Neither of them had been to Europe before, but Lila's mother had given them a surprisingly generous check, and they said to each other: why not?

They started out in Normandy, and their first night there, as they sat puzzling over the menu, a man approached them. He was an English civil servant on holiday. "Excuse me," he said, "I overheard you and your wife speaking English, and I wonder if I might ask an enormous favor of you."

The favor was to cash a personal check — the hotel in the village was being sticky for some reason. Robert agreed to cash it — it was only for fifty pounds — but with some concern. The world, after all, was full of con artists with trustworthy faces, and one couldn't be too careful.

The check went through, however, with no trouble, and the Englishman now sends Robert and Lila Christmas greetings every year. He signs them with a joint signature — Nigel and Jane — and adds a few words about the weather, the state of their health (both his and Jane's) and then thanks them yet again for coming to their rescue in Normandy. This has been going on now for twenty-five years.

Lila's grandfather was William White Westfield, the prosperous Toronto lawyer, who, in the twenties, wrote a series of temperance novels that were printed by a church-owned press and distributed free to libraries across Ontario.

When Robert married Lila, her mother's wedding gift was

a set of these books — this, of course, was in addition to the honeymoon check. "Even if you never read them, Robert," she said, "I know you'll be amused by the titles."

He was. *Journey to Sobriety, The Good Wife's Victory, A Farewell to Inner Cravings* and, his favorite, *Tom Taylor, Battles and Bottles*. Robert and Lila displayed the books in a little bookcase that Robert made out of bricks and plain pine boards. It gave their apartment a look of solidarity, a glow. They lived, when they were first married, in an old duplex just north of High Park that had three rooms, all painted in deep postwar colors — a purple kitchen, a Wedgwood-blue bedroom, and a Williamsburg-green living room. That winter they sanded the living room floor by hand. Later, this became their low-water mark: "Remember when we were so broke we couldn't afford to rent a floor sander." It took them a whole month, square foot by square foot, to sand their way through the sticky old varnish. Robert, who was preparing for exams, remembers how he would study for an hour — memorizing the names of the cranial nerves or whatever — and then sand for an hour.

When they finished at last with the sanding and with the five coats of wax, and when Robert had passed his examinations, they bought a bottle of cheap wine, and sat in the middle of the shining floor drinking it. Lila lifted her glass toward the shelf of temperance books and said, "Cheers."

"Cheers" was what Nigel and Jane had written on their first Christmas card. Just a simple "Cheers, and again our hearty thanks."

The next winter they wrote, or rather Nigel wrote, "A damp winter, but we've settled into our new house and find it comfortable."

By coincidence, Robert and Lila had moved as well — to a new apartment that had an elevator and was closer to the hospital where Robert was interning. Thinking of Nigel and Jane and their many other friends, Lila arranged to have the mail forwarded to the new address. She missed the old duplex, especially the purple kitchen with its high curving cornices. She suspected Robert of having a cyst of ambition, hard as a nut. She was right. This made her feel lonely and gave her a primal sense of deprivation, but she heard in her head a voice saying that the deprivation was deserved.

It was only at night, when she and Robert lay in each other's arms, that everything slipped back into its proper place. Her skin became mysteriously feathered, like an owl's or some other fast-flying night bird. "Open, open," she begged the dark air of their little bedroom, and often it did.

It was different for Robert, who felt himself settling into marriage like a traveler without provisions. Sleeping with Lila in the first year of their marriage, he often thought: How can I use this moment? What can it teach me?

But finally he let himself be persuaded that he had come under the power of love, and that he was helpless.

Robert and Lila had a baby that was stillborn. It must not be thought of as a tragedy, friends told them; it was nature's way of weeding out the imperfect. They left soon afterward for three weeks in England because they were persuaded that a change of scene would do them good. The flight was very long, but smooth. Fresh Canadian blueberries were served on the plane, and all the passengers piled off, smiling at each other with blue teeth. "We should get in touch with Nigel and Jane," said Lila with her blue mouth.

But when they tried to find them in the telephone book, they discovered they weren't listed. There was nothing to be done. The Christmas cards had carried no return address, only a London postmark, and so Robert and Lila were forced to admit defeat. Both of them were more disappointed than they said.

The year before, Nigel had written: "Our garden gives us great pleasure." Lila had felt envious and wished she had a garden to give her pleasure.

Both Lila and Robert liked to stay in bed on Sunday morning and make love, but occasionally, four or five times a year, they went to church. There was pleasure to be had in passing through a set of wide oak doors into the calm carpeted Protestant sanctuary, and they enjoyed singing the familiar old hymns, Robert for their simple melodies and Lila for their shapely words which seemed to meet in the final verse like a circle completed. "Reclothe me in my rightful mind," was a phrase she loved, but was puzzled by. What was her rightful mind? All autumn she'd wondered.

At Christmas, the card from England came zipping through the mail slot with the message, "An exceptional winter. Our pond has frozen over completely, and Jane has taken up ice skating, North-American style."

Robert read the message over several times. Each inky letter was crisply formed and the Ts were crossed with merry little banners. "How can they have a pond if they live in London?" he asked. He was thinking about Jane, imagining her whirling and dashing to and fro in a sky-blue skating costume and showing a pronounced roundness of thigh.

"Do you have any recollection at all of what Nigel looked like?" Lila asked Robert once, but Robert couldn't remember anything about him except that he had looked respectable and solid, and not much older than himself. Neither of them could remember Jane at all.

Lila took a job teaching in a French school, but quit six weeks later when she discovered she was pregnant. Twin boys were born. They were exquisite, lively and responsive, following with their quick little eyes and the faces of their parents, the turning blades of a butterfly mobile and bright lights of all kinds. Robert and Lila carried them into the big chilly Protestant church one rainy Sunday and had them officially christened. The little house they rented filled up overnight with the smell of talcum powder and oats cooking; Robert became an improbable night visitor who smelled dark and cold in his overcoat. From across the ocean came the message: "Summer found us back in Normandy, reliving old memories."

"Where does the time go?" Robert said one morning in a

voice that was less a lament than a cry of accomplishment. It seemed to him a good thing for time to pass quickly. He wondered sometimes, when he went off in the mornings, especially in the winter, if work wasn't just a way of coping with time. He also wondered, without jealousy or malice, what kind of salary Nigel pulled down.

They were surprised at how quickly routines and habits accrued. Patterns, rhythms, ways of doing things — they evolved without a need for conscious decision. The labor of the household split itself, not equitably, perhaps, but neatly. Robert ruled over the garage and the cement-lined kingdom of the basement, keeping an ear permanently cocked for the murmuring of machinery and for its occasional small failures. For Lila there was the house, the children, the bills and the correspondence. The task of writing Christmas cards fell mainly to her. One year she sat down at Grandfather Westfield's roll-top desk and wrote 175 cards. So many friends, so many acquaintances! Still she paused, lifted her head and melo-dramatically said to herself, "I am a lonely woman." She wished once again that she knew Nigel and Jane's address so she could send them a snap of the boys and ask them if they had any children — she suspected they didn't, in which case she would like to write them a few words of comfort, perhaps counsel patience.

Nigel had written that year about the coal strike, about a fortnight he and Jane had spent in Scotland, about the flooding of a river near their house.

Eight people were seated around a table. There were candles. Lila had made a salmon mousse and surrounded it with cucumber slices and, after that, there was a leg of lamb, wild rice and fresh asparagus. Robert walked around the table and poured wine. The conversation had taken a curious turn, with each couple recounting the story of their honeymoon. Some of the stories were touched-up sexual burlesques — the red wine brought a slice of the ribald to the table — and some were confused, unedited accounts of misunderstandings or revelations.

Robert and Lila described their month in France, and Robert, making a fine story of it, told the others about the check they had cashed for an English stranger who now sends them Christmas cards.

"And I've saved every single one of them," Lila said.

This surprised Robert, who was proud to be married to a woman who was not a collector of trivia. Lila sent him a wide, apologetic smile across the roasted lamb and a shrug that said: Isn't it absurd, the things we do.

"You took a real chance," someone at the table remarked. "You could have lost the whole bundle."

Robert nodded, agreeing. He thought again as he had thought before, how generous, open and trusting he and Lila must have been in those days. It was an image he cherished, the two of them, lost in their innocence and in each other.

Lila went to visit her mother one day and they had a quarrel. The argument was over something of no importance, a photograph Lila had misplaced. They both apologized afterward, but Lila cried on her way out to the parking lot, and a man stopped her and said, "Pardon me. You seem to be in distress. May I help you."

He had a kind, anonymous face. Lila told him she was upset because she had quarreled with someone. The man understood her to mean she had quarreled with a lover, and that was what Lila intended him to understand.

He walked her to her car, held her arm for a moment and said a few kind words. Things would look different in the morning. Things had a way of blowing over. Misunderstandings were inevitable, but sometimes they yielded a deeper sense of the other person.

Lila drove home in that state of benign suspension which can occur when a complete stranger surprises one by an act of intimacy. She felt not only rescued, but deserving of rescue.

Often, she thought how it would be possible to tell Nigel things she could never tell Robert. He would never drum his fingers on the table or interrupt or correct her. He would be patient, attentive and filled with a tender regard for women.

She seldom thought about him concretely, but an impression of him beat at the back of her head, a pocket watch ticking against a silky lining. "Jane has made a splendid recovery," he wrote rather mysteriously at Christmas.

"A wonderful year," Lila wrote to friends at Christmas. "The children are growing so fast."

When she wrote such things, she wondered what happened to all the other parts of her life that could not be satisfyingly annotated. She tried at first to rescue them with a series of graceful, old-fashioned observations, but she soon became tired and discouraged and suspected herself of telling lies.

Robert and Lila acquired a cat, which ran up a tree in a nearby park and refused to come down. "He'll come down when he's good and hungry," Lila assured her children, but several days passed and still the cat refused to descend. At length, Robert dipped a broomstick into a tin of tuna fish and, standing on a ladder, managed to coax the cat down by waving this fragrant wand before his stubborn nose.

A photographer for a Toronto newspaper happened to be standing not ten feet away, and he snapped a picture of Robert in the act of rescue. The picture and story were picked up by a wire service as a human-interest piece a few days later — this was during a quiet spell between elections and hijackings — and appeared on the inside pages of newspapers across the continent. Robert was amazed. He was, he realized, mildly famous, perhaps as famous as he would ever be again. It was not the kind of fame he had imagined for himself and, in fact, he was a little ashamed of the whole episode. Friends phoned from distant cities and congratulated him on his act of heroism. "Yes," Lila said with expansive good humor, "I am indeed married to the illustrious cat rescuer."

Robert couldn't help wondering if the picture had been published in the English dailies, and if Jane had seen it. It might have made her laugh. Jane, Jane. He imagined she was a woman who laughed easily. "Jane and I are both in excellent spirits," a recent Christmas greeting had reported.

Whenever Lila went into a café or restaurant, she slipped the little packets of sugar into her purse, even though she and Robert no longer used sugar. They had grown health-conscious. Robert swam laps twice a week at the sports club he joined, and he was making an effort to cut down on martinis. All this dieting and exercise had stripped away his flesh so that when they made love Lila felt his hip bones grinding on hers. She believed she should feel healthier than she did, what with all the expensive, fresh vegetables she carried home and cooked in the special little steamer Robert had brought back from San Francisco.

She wondered if Jane had to watch her figure as carefully as she herself did. She wondered if Jane were attractive. Sometimes, she saw women on the street, women who had a look of Englishness about them, someone wearing a simple linen dress or with straight graying hair. If these women wore perfume, it was something grassy. They were determinedly cheerful; they put a smiling face on everything, keeping life joyful, keeping it puffing along, keeping away from its dark edges. They swallowed their disappointments as though to do so was part of a primordial bargain.

"Jane and I are seriously considering a walking tour of the Hebrides next year," Nigel had written.

Robert applied for a year off in order to do some research on the immune system, but almost from the start things went badly. The data he required accumulated slowly and yielded little that was specific. He learned too late that someone else, someone younger and with a larger grant, was on the same track at Stanford. He insisted on being given computer time in order to correlate his findings, and then discovered he was painfully, helplessly inept at using a computer. He began drifting to his club in the early afternoons to swim laps, or sometimes he drank in the bar and told Lila that he swam laps. His disappointment, his difficulty, his lies, his drunkenness, his life sliding away from him down a long blind chute, made him decide that the time had come to buy a house.

The house was expensive, ten rooms of glass and dark-stained wood cunningly perched on the side of a ravine, but it saved his life, or so he said at the time. He and Lila and the boys moved in at the end of November. As always, when they moved, Lila made careful, tactful, heroic efforts to have their mail forwarded. She looked forward to the barrage of Christmas greetings. Nigel and Jane's card came from the Hebrides that year, just a short note saying, "We made it at last. The birds are magnificent."

Lila had the use of her mother's summer cottage in Muskoka, and she and Robert and the children liked to spend four or five weeks there every summer. There was a particular nightgown she wore at the lake. It was altogether different from her city nightgowns, which were long, sliplike things in shiny materials and in colors such as ivory or melon or plum. The cottage nightgown was white cotton printed with quite large red poppies. There was a ruffle at the neck and another at the feet. On a bigger woman, it would have been comic; it was large, loose, a balloon of a garment.

Robert couldn't imagine where it had come from. It was difficult to think of someone as elegant as Lila actually going out to buy such a thing. She kept it in an old drawer at the cottage, and one summer they arrived and found that a family of mice had built a nest in its flower-strewn folds. The children ran screaming.

"Throw it away," Robert told her.

But she had washed it in the lake with strong detergent and dried it in the sun. "As good as new," she said after she mended one small hole.

For a week the children called it her mouse gown and refused to touch it.

But Robert loved her in it. How he loved her! The wet, lakey smell was in her hair all summer long, and on her skin. She was his shining girl again, easy and ardent and restored to innocence.

Summer was one thing, but for most of the year Lila and Robert lived in a country too cold for park benches or *al fresco* dining or cuddling on yachts or unzipping the spirit. They suffered a climate more suitable for sobering insights, for guilt, for the entrenchment of broad streams of angst and darkness.

England, too, was a cold country, yet Nigel wrote: "We've had a cheerless autumn and no summer to speak of, but as long as Jane and I have our books and a good fire, we can't complain."

Just as heavy drinkers gather at parties to condemn others for overindulgence, so Lila lovingly gathered stories of wrecked marriages and nervous breakdowns — as though an accumulation of statistics might guard her sanity and her marriage, as if the sheer weight of disaster would prevent the daily erosion of what she had once called her happiness. She wailed, loudly and frequently, about the numbers of her friends who popped Valium or let their marriages slide into boredom. "I'll go crazy if I hear about one more divorce." She said this mournfully, but with a sly edge of triumph. Her friends' children were taking drugs or running away from home. She could weep, she told Robert, when she looked around and saw the wreckage of human lives.

But she didn't weep. She was, if anything, reaffirmed by disaster. "I ran into Bess Carrier downtown," she told Robert, "and she looked about sixty, completely washed out, devastated. You wouldn't have known her. It was heartbreaking. I get so depressed sometimes. There must be something we can do for her."

Robert knew it would come to nothing, Lila's plans to take Bess Carrier out for lunch or send her flowers or invite her around for a drink. Lila's charity seldom got past the point of corpse-counting these days; it seemed to take most of her time.

No one escaped her outraged pity — except perhaps Nigel and Jane. They were safe, across the ocean, locked into their seasonal rhythms, consumed by their various passions. They were taking Portuguese lessons, they had written. And growing orchids.

Lila loved parties, and she and Robert went to a great many. But when they drove home past lighted houses and streets full of parked cars, she was tormented by the parties she had missed, assuming, as a matter of course, that these briefly glimpsed gatherings glittered with a brighter and kinder light. She imagined rooms fragrant with woodsmoke and fine food — and talk that was both grave and charming. Who could guess what her imagination had cost her over the years?

The same plunging sense of loss struck her each year when she opened the Christmas greeting from Nigel and Jane. Elsewhere, these cards said to her, people were able to live lives of deep trust. How had it happened — that others were able to inhabit their lives with such grace and composure?

"He probably sends out thousands of these things," Robert once said to Lila, who was deeply offended. "He must be a bit off his rocker. He must be a real nut."

It was the month of July. Robert bundled the boys into the station wagon and they drove across the country, camping, climbing in the mountains, cooking eggs and coffee over an open fire, breathing fresh air. Lila went to Rome on a tour with a group from the art gallery. While she was gone, her mother died of heart failure on the platform of the College Street subway station. The moment she collapsed, her straw hat flying into the air, was the same moment when Lila stood in the nave of St. Peter's, looked up into its magisterial vaulting and felt that she had asked too much of life. Like Nigel and Jane, she must try to find a simpler way of being: playing word games at the kitchen table, being attentive to changes in the weather, taking an interest in local history, or perhaps collecting seashells on a beach, taking each one into her hand and minutely examining its color and pattern.

A snowy day. Lila was at home. There was a fire, a pot of Earl Grey and Beethoven being monumentally unpleasant on the record player. She turned the music off and was rewarded by a blow of silence. In the whole of the long afternoon there was not one interruption, not even a phone call. At seven, Robert arrived home and the peace was broken by this peaceful man.

A snowy day. Robert was up at seven. Granola in a bowl given to him by his wife. She was lost in a dream. He would like to have surprised her by saying something startling, but he was convinced, prematurely as it turned out, that certain rhythms of speech had left him forever. He knew this just as he knew that he was unlikely ever again to kiss the inner elbow of a woman and behave foolishly.

A snowy day. Nigel wrote: "We are wrapped in a glorious blizzard, an extraordinary North Pole of a day. Jane and I send good wishes. May you have peace, joy and blessings of every kind."

Loss of faith came at inappropriate times, settling on the brain like a coat of deadly lacquer. Lila thought of her dead baby. Robert thought of his abandoned research. But, luckily, seasonal tasks kept the demons down — the porch to open and clean, the storm windows to see to, the leaves. Robert and Lila always gave a party for the staff in the fall. After the fall party, there were the Christmas things to be done. The children were doing well in school. Soon it would be summer.

Occasionally, in a crowd, in an airport or a restaurant or in the street, Robert would see a woman's face so prepared in its openness for the appeal of passion, tenderness or love, so composed and ready, that he was moved to drop everything and take her in his arms. A thousand times he had been able to resist. Once he had not.

She was a woman not much younger than Lila and not as pretty. His feeling for her was intense and complicated. He was corrupted by the wish to make her happy, and the fact that it took little to make her happy touched him in the same way his children's simple wants had once aroused his extravagant generosity. He had no idea why he loved her. She rode a bicycle and pulled her hair back with a ribbon. Her hair ribbons, her candor, her books and records, and especially her strong rounded arms, put him in mind of Jane. When she closed a book she was reading, she marked her place with a little silk cord and folded her hands, one inside the other, in exactly the same way he imagined Jane would do.

Lila was stepping into a taxi on her way to see her lawyer. Nothing she could do, not even the bold, off-hand way she swung her handbag on her shoulder, could hide the touching awkwardness and clumsy surprise of a woman who had been betrayed by someone she loves.

The taxi driver drove through the late-afternoon traffic. "Would you object if I smoke?" he asked Lila, who was embarrassed by his courtesy. She wondered if he had a wife. His shoulder-length hair was clean and more than commonly fine, and on the fingers of his left hand there were three rings, so large and intricate and so brilliantly colored that she was moved to comment on them.

"I go with a girl who did a jewelry course in New Brunswick," he said. "She keeps making me rings. I don't know what I'm going to do if she keeps making me rings."

"Are you going to marry her?" Lila asked. Now that she was taking the first step to dissolve her marriage, she felt she had the right to ask all manner of outrageous questions.

"Marriage?" He paid grave attention to her question. "I don't know about marriage. Marriage is a pretty long haul."

"Yes, it is," Lila said. She rolled down the window and looked at the heavy, late-afternoon sky which seemed now to form a part of her consciousness. Why wouldn't someone help her? She slumped, turned her face sideways and bit on the bitter vinyl of the upholstery. "Nigel, Nigel," her heart pleaded.

Robert missed his house, he missed his sons and often he missed Lila. Guilt might explain the trembling unease he felt when he stamped the snow off his shoes and rang the bell of what had been his front door. Inside he would find the smell of fresh coffee, that most forgiving of smells, and the spicy chalk smell of adolescent boys. And what else? — the teasing drift of Lila's perfume, a scent that reminded him of grass.

He arrived at 9:00 A.M. every Saturday, insisting, he said rather quaintly, on doing the household chores. More often than not these chores consisted of tapping on the furnace gauge or putting a listening ear under the hood of Lila's car or filling out some forms for the fire insurance. He did all these things with a good — some would say guilty — heart. He even offered to do the Christmas cards and advise their many, many friends that he and Lila were now separated.

Most of the friends replied with short notes of condolence. Several of them said, "We know what you're going through." Some said, "Perhaps you'll find a way to work things out." One of them, Bess Carrier, wrote, "We've suspected for some time that things weren't right."

Nigel wrote: "We hope this Christmas finds you both joyous and eager for the new year. Time goes so quickly, but Jane and I often think of the two of you, so happy and young in Normandy, and how you found the goodness to come to our aid."

Lila missed Robert, but she didn't miss him all the time. At first, she spent endless hours shopping; all around her, in the department stores, in the boutiques, people were grabbing for the things they wanted. What did she want, she asked herself, sitting before a small fire in the evening and fingering the corduroy of the slipcover. She didn't know.

She rearranged the house, put a chair at an angle, had the piano moved so that the sun struck its polished top. She carried her Grandfather Westfield's temperance novels out of the basement and arranged them on a pretty little table, using a piece of quartz for a book end. The stone scratched the finish, but she rubbed it with a bit of butter as her mother used to do, and forgot about it. Some days she woke up feeling as light as a girl, and as blameless. The lightness stayed with her all day, and she served her sons plates of soup and sandwiches for dinner. When summer came, she bought herself a pair of white cotton pants and a number of boyish T-shirts. One of them had a message across the front that said "Birds are people too."

She had a great many friends, most of them women, and sometimes it seemed to her that she spent all day talking to these women friends. She wondered now and then how Jane filled her days, if she knitted or visited the sick or what. She wished they could meet. She would tell Jane everything. She would trust her absolutely.

Certain kinds of magazines are filled with articles on how to catch a man and how, having caught him, to keep him happy, keep him faithful, keep him amorous. But Lila and her friends talked mainly about how few men were worth catching and how fewer still were worth keeping. Yet, when Robert asked if he might come back, she agreed.

She would have expected a woman in her situation to feel victorious, but she felt only a crush of exhaustion that had the weight and sound of continuous rain. Robert suggested they get away for a vacation, somewhere hot: Spain or Portugal. (Nigel and Jane had gone to Portugal where they had spent many hours walking on the beaches.)

Lila said: "Maybe next year." She was too tired to think about packing a suitcase, but next year she was bound to have more energy.

Robert gave Lila an opal ring. Lila gave Robert a set of scuba equipment. Robert gave Lila a book of French poems that he'd found at a garage sale. Lila gave Robert a soft scarf of English wool and put it around his neck and patted it in place, saying, "Merry Christmas."

"Merry Christmas," Robert said back, and to himself he said: There's no place in the world I would rather be at this minute.

The card from England was late, but the buff envelope was reassuringly familiar and so was the picture — a scenic view of Salisbury Plain under a wafery layer of snow. Inside, Nigel had written: "Jane has been in a coma for some months now, but it is a comfort to me that she is not in pain and that she perhaps hears a little of what goes on about her."

Lila read the words several times before they swam into comprehension. Then she phoned Robert at his office, and he slumped forward, put a fist to his forehead and closed his eyes thinking: *Jane, Jane.* "How can he bear this," Lila said several times. *Nigel.*

They sat together in a corner of the quiet living room. A clock ticked on the wall. This room, like the other rooms in the house, was filled with airy furniture and thick rugs. Fragile curtains framed a window that looked out onto a wooded ravine, and beyond the ravine could be seen the tops of apartment buildings. From the triple-paned windows of these apartments one could glimpse a pale sky scratched with weather whorls, and a broad lake that joined, eventually, a wide gray river whose water emptied into the Atlantic Ocean. As oceans go, this was a mild and knowable ocean, with friendly coasts rising smoothly out of the waves and leading directly to white roads, forests and the jointed streets of foreign towns and villages. Both Robert and Lila, each enclosed in a separate vision, could imagine houses filled with lighted rooms, and these rooms — like the one they were sitting in — were softened by the presence of furniture, curtains, carpets, men and women and children, and by that curious human contrivance that binds them together.

They know after all this time about love — that it's dim and unreliable and little more than a reflection on the wall. It is also capricious, idiotic, sentimental, imperfect and inconstant, and most often seems to be the exclusive preserve of others. Sitting in a room that was slowly growing dark, they found themselves wishing they could measure its pure anchoring force or account for its random visitations. Of course they could not — which was why, after a time, they began to talk about other things: the weather, would it snow, would the wind continue its bitter course, would the creek freeze over, would there be another power cut, what would happen during the night.